VENTURE CAPITALIST
FORBIDDEN *Love*

ISBN-13: 978-1-9802-6614-3
Venture Capitalist: Forbidden Love/Ainsley St Claire—1st edition

AINSLEY ST CLAIRE

VENTURE CAPITALIST
FORBIDDEN *Love*

A Novel

EMERSON

I wasn't supposed to fall in love with him. I wasn't supposed to need him. I wasn't supposed to want him. But I did fall in love with him, I do need him, and I most certainly want him.

In the beginning...

I CAN'T BELIEVE that today of all days I'm running late. I'm usually never late. I live the mantra that late is if you aren't at your destination fifteen minutes before scheduled time. Ugh!

Running into the new office in downtown San Francisco, I am greeted by a well put-together receptionist at Sullivan Healy Newhouse, often referred to as SHN. We're the preeminent venture capital firm in the Bay Area. As of last Friday afternoon, they purchased my company, Clear Professional Services, and I'm now joining the firm as a partner to manage the professional services of all their investment start-ups. It's a way to have a steady paycheck and work with some of the brightest people in San Francisco and the Bay Area.

The offices are bright and open with sparkling clear glass walls, leather office chairs in bright colors, white shellacked desks and tables, and bamboo wooden floors helping to give the space a clean and sharp look. Exiting the elevators, I introduce myself to the receptionist. "Hi. My name is Emerson Winthrop. I'm supposed to meet Sara White."

Smiling, she stands from behind her desk in a soft blue skirt suit that meets just above her knees, a black patterned silk blouse and a soft blue matching jacket. Her highlighted blonde hair is up in a tight chignon, and her jewelry is tasteful yet expensive. Reaching out, she shakes my hand and says, "Welcome, Emerson. I'm Annabel Ryan. We're happy to have you here at SHN. I'll let Sara know you're here." She makes the call and alerts Sara of my arrival, then tells her she's going to bring me back to her office with a detour by the company break room. "Emerson, follow me. We'll grab coffee and breakfast, and I'll walk you back to Sara's office."

I saw the break room during the process of SHN buying my company; it was impressive then and even more so now. Located in the center of the office, it hosts coffee machines that make coffees, teas, different cocoas, and ciders, an espresso machine where you can make your own, and also a Nespresso machine. Lined atop white Caesarstone counters, there doesn't seem to be any escape from caffeine should anyone desire it. Next to the sink is a glass-fronted Sub-Zero refrigerator stuffed with sodas, juices, waters, fresh fruit and vegetables. Open shelving on the walls gives the kitchen a giant pantry feel with each floor-to-ceiling shelf containing unending rows of almost every snack you can imagine.

In the center, an island which stores all the various plates, silverware, chopsticks, napkins and a food buffet. This morning's breakfast food selection includes various fruit salad selections, bagels, pastries, a cheese plate and a warming plate with eggs and bacon. I'm awestruck. "Is this the spread every day?"

"Unfortunately for my waistline, yes. The guys can eat like crazy, though most of us girls here don't have the metabolism to eat like this. I usually bring in my own coffee so I'm not tempted. Lunch is catered every day and arrives about noon. There is a menu on the fridge so you'll know if you want to bring something in from home. And for those working late, there's a light dinner brought in most evenings." She reminds me of Vanna White as she points out the various amenities. "In the fridge is an assortment of sodas and beers. If we don't carry your favorite, let me know and we'll stock it."

I fill my cup with pure black coffee and an artificial sweetener and follow Annabel to meet with Sara. She's the corporate counsel and currently runs all the operations at SHN. I'll be taking all the human resources and talent pieces off her plate. She's my peer and the only other female partner. During the purchase, we bonded, part of the reason I chose to sell to SHN.

Sara stands and approaches me with open arms. "Emerson! I'm so thrilled you're here." We make polite chitchat, and then she hands me a calendar for the day. It tells me I'll spend the morning with her going through paperwork, have lunch with the partners, and then I'll be with one of the partners in the afternoon—Dillon Healy.

Before I know it, the morning is gone, even though the real part of my onboarding paperwork was taken care of last week in the lawyer's offices when I sold my company for three times its value. All ten of my employees are transitioning this morning, too, but they all work remotely. Honestly, my business was small potatoes compared to the deals SHN works, but it was a lot to me.

Over the past five years, I grew Clear Professional Services into a dominating provider of all the back-office things small- and mid-sized businesses need, but may not want to do here in Silicon Valley and beyond. We handle billing and accounts receivable, accounts payable, manage the HR function which includes recruitment, and our goal is to never say no when a client asks for something for their business.

Sara and I walk over to lunch to stretch our legs and enjoy a bit of the rare sunshine. "I love this area, but I sure do miss the sunshine," Sara admits.

"It's getting hot out in the desert. It'll bring the fog in, and summer will be gone. Tell me how things are going with your new boyfriend... Henry, was it?"

Blushing, she shares, "He's great. It's still new, but it was unprofessional of me to tell you about him. Please don't let the guys know I said anything. They are very particular that our personal lives should remain personal."

"I understand. It will be our secret. But tell me about Henry. I have no social life, so I need to live vicariously through you."

"He's positively wonderful. I've never been able to be so free and open with anyone like I am with him. He works for a start-up down in Palo Alto."

"Sara! I don't want his stats, I want his *stats!* Is he a good kisser? Does he make you feel all gooey inside?"

Sara blushes a deep shade of pink, which turns even her ears. "He does. He has this way of making me feel good about myself but also seems to want to hear my opinions and ideas. We're moving fast, but we both agree this is pretty great."

I squeeze her arm. "That sounds amazing. I'll admit, I am a bit jealous, but it gives me some hope that there are still some decent guys out there."

We arrive at the trendy waterfront restaurant and are shown to a private room, where the three other partners are waiting for us.

DILLON

SARA AND EMERSON walk into the meeting, the girls both look amazing. I played with Sara before she joined the firm, but she wanted more from me than that. It had been a mistake, and thankfully only Mason, one of the other partners, figured it out; however, we almost lost Sara and her partnership because of it, which would have been devastating. Though looking at the two women now, I can't help but briefly fantasize about the three of us together.

Emerson is beautiful. She's tall and also wears a significant heel, which puts her over six feet. I love her blonde hair cascading down her back below her shoulder blades. The slit in her black pencil skirt is demure enough, work appropriate, but at the same time it makes me want to peek underneath to see what she's wearing. Her silk cream blouse with a black velvet trim is sexy in a librarian way.

"Ladies, welcome. Please have a seat." We put Emerson at the head of the table and order a bottle of 1992 Screaming Eagle Cabernet Sauvignon. It's expensive, but we're excited to have Emerson as part of our team. We toast to her joining us.

It wasn't an easy sell at the beginning. Emerson had put together an interesting concept, and she didn't need us. Her company would do all the business management for various hot start-ups across the bay area and a few other tech hubs across the country—pay bills, recruit, stock option management, manage building issues and anything else that keeps the start-up from doing what they're supposed to be doing.

Before meeting Emerson, I remember someone talking at a party about the business management concept, and I didn't understand the value. Now I know that all those things are part of running a business, and it's certainly beneficial for someone else to deal with it.

In the last three years, we became the most sought-after venture capital firm in the Bay Area. Mason has an MBA from Harvard with an uncanny ability to understand the business side and positioning for sale or going public, Cameron brings a strong technology background to the table, and I bring the knowledge of the numbers. All three of us met at Stanford as undergrads. We were recruited by various start-ups out of school, and we lucked out with all three going huge, making us extremely wealthy very young.

We began our funding of start-ups together as a hobby and a way to share some of our luck, giving seed money to projects we liked as a side gig to our jobs. When four of our investments were bought for millions of dollars each, we were addicted to the gamble and the high of identifying a winner when investing in an exciting idea. Don't get me wrong, not everything we invested in has been successful, but our hit rate has been pretty high, and we like to get in early.

Sara was our company attorney at a law firm we used. We hung our shingle as Sullivan Healy Newhouse, or SHN, about three years ago and hired Sara out of the law firm, offering her partnership. Now we have close to fifty employees helping with the various start-ups and investigating up-and-coming trends. However, we knew something was missing, though we couldn't figure out what it was.

Then we watched a few of our start-ups not make it because they seemed to get bogged down in the operations side of the business and were no longer doing what they were supposed to be doing. It was then that I understood why a professional services company appeared to be a solution.

We're regulars at the Venture Capital Silicon Valley Summit. It offers concepts and start-ups an opportunity to present their ideas and business plans to venture capital firms and individuals. Each is looking at various kinds of funding and are hoping some will invest in their ideas and help make them realities—and the owners very wealthy.

During the conference, we usually sat in private rooms and met with potential investments. I'd never paid attention to nor attended any of the breakout sessions. Randomly, Emerson's talk on "How to Do What You Do Best Without Complications" caught my eye. It seemed to call to me, so I decided to hear what she had to say. I arrived a few minutes late and sat in the back with no expectations.

She was not only a knockout in her conservative black suit with a soft pink blouse and high-heeled black pumps, but she was smart. And not just smart—she was brilliant. Emerson gave an insightful presentation and answered question after question.

She could speak to managing accounts receivable and multiple human resources issues, and her pet saying, "How to see the forest for the trees," hit home for me. I knew she was someone I could work with, so I collected all the marketing materials she had and brought them back to the team. They could hear my enthusiasm for what she could bring to our investments to make them stronger and better.

We put our research team on her and her company, and it seemed to be a no-brainer. At least for us.

I reached out to her with a request for coffee, and she politely brushed me off. She ducked my calls and emails for two months. I felt like a dog in heat when she finally agreed to meet me. Apparently, she had four other VC firms looking at her. I knew it was going to be tricky, mostly because she had no interest in selling. It took constant calls before she finally agreed to talk over the phone. My team shared our feelings that we would all benefit by working together. Sure, we could create it, but she had already worked out the kinks, and she was magnetic and would be a great asset to our team.

We went into full buy-mode with her. We invited her to the offices, and again she put us off. We sent her flowers and still no response. Before we could give up, our marketing team suggested we send a crate of oranges to her office with a note written by Mason, as the managing partner, asking "Can you squeeze us in?" She sent back a photo of her and a few members of her team drinking orange juice with a time and their address. The meeting was finally going to happen.

She impressed us all with her negotiation skills. When we got a look at her profit and loss statements, we were pleasantly surprised. She was extremely profitable and would be bringing a significant amount of business as well as ten employees across the Bay Area, plus one in San Antonio. She wasn't negotiating for herself, but we liked that she wanted to look out for her team. It took six months, but finally she and her team joined SHN.

Conversation during today's lunch was fun. We all laughed as Cameron shared a story about his weekend, getting stranded in a biker bar in Sacramento and being hit on by one of the biker's girlfriends. Apparently it was a mess, but he now has new fans in Sac.

We talked about a partner retreat, some business issues, and what we have pending. The two-and-a-half-hour lunch was an excellent start to our working relationship.

San Francisco is my favorite city. The City, as it's referred to by the locals, is simply urban. Tall concrete buildings in an exact grid pattern, the grass saved for parks and the occasional backyard. Ever-present skyscrapers are smudged by the haze-filled sky, offering no direct sunlight and few birds. Cars race between red traffic lights, stubbornly flickering in their gray surroundings.

Sara decides she can't walk the eight blocks again in her shoes and chooses to ride back with Cameron and Mason to the office, who extend the offer to Emerson. Peering between the buildings at the cloudless skies and taking a deep breath, she says, "It's such a beautiful day. Dillon, we don't meet for another half hour. I think I'd like to walk back. Do you mind if I meet you back at the office?"

Surprised at her passing up a ride, I tell her, "I would be happy to walk with you."

Despite the three-inch heels, she's confident in herself. I can tell by her powerful stride, the way she holds her head up and her shoulders back.

As we walk, we make idle chitchat. "Where are you from originally?" she asks.

With my hands in my pockets, I walk and turn to her at the same time. "Just outside Detroit. What about you?"

"Denver. It's probably why I miss the sun so much. We tend to have more sunshine than San Diego."

"Summers are brutal here. The hot desert valley brings fog, gray and cold to San Francisco. How long have you lived here?"

"I moved to Palo Alto for undergrad and then went east to law school. After graduating almost eight years ago, I came back. And you?"

"I moved here when I was eighteen—which was a long time ago—to attend Stanford and never left."

There were people everywhere. Panhandlers, business suits, the workout-clad and tons of tourist with cameras. We dodged them all like salmon running upstream.

"Do you have any brothers or sisters?" she asks.

"I have a younger sister. How about you?"

"I have four brothers. I'm the baby."

"Four? Wow! That must have been crazy growing up."

"Any guy who looked at me would get the evil eye, and if he talked to me, they might take him out. Made me undesirable to boys while growing up."

"Are they all still in Denver?"

"Yes. All married with at least three kids. What about your sister?"

"She lives in Texas and is married but no kids yet. I'm expecting a call anytime now. She's a teacher, and my brotherin-law works for a big insurance company. They live to focus on their family."

"I suppose that's the way it should be."

We enter the building and I hold the door to the elevator. "You're probably right. Meet you in my office in fifteen minutes?"

EMERSON

I KNOW MOST PEOPLE find Dillon intimidating. He's over 6'5", and I believe he played football at Stanford close to the same time I was there. With sandy blond hair and piercing emerald-green eyes, he is by all means incredibly attractive. I've never seen him as intimidating. He reminds me of my brothers—funny in a self-deprecating way. I find myself surprised by how comfortable I am with him.

He has several clients who need my attention. When we return, I grab a pad of paper and a pen and meet him in his office.

He looks at me with a puzzled expression. "You do have a tablet, don't you?"

"Yes, but I'm a bit old-school and prefer to write everything down on paper. I tend to remember the information better."

He seems puzzled by this, but lets it go. "Okay then, write away. The first company we need to get you in with is Accurate Software."

Picking up the phone, he calls the founder and sets up a time for us to come by tomorrow, then proceeds to tell me about the company while handing me a three-inch folder of due diligence and research which is pretty specific. It includes information on each employee and notes on a few who may not be a good fit for the culture they are starting to build. We spend the afternoon talking about what they've done both successfully and not so successfully. We will be meeting with Accurate Software, as well as three other companies this week.

When I look up, it's after seven. It has been a long and exhausting day which has gone by in a flash.

"Oh, it's late, and I should get going. I have a dog at home which my dog walker let out about five hours ago. I may have quite the mess on my hands if I don't get home soon."

"Can I give you a ride home?" he offers.

It's thoughtful, but I can tell he's going to be trouble for me. Without a second thought, I tell him, "I can grab Muni."

In a protective voice, he insists, "You can't take the bus home at this hour."

"Dillon, I take the bus all the time. It's what people do in a big city. I'll be fine."

"I'll drive you home."

"I live out in the Avenues in a bungalow. It's too far for you."

"Nonsense! I'll meet you by the elevators in ten minutes and drive you home."

I hold my hands up to give up the fight. "Okay. See you in ten minutes."

As we drive out of downtown, I direct him to my small home in the Presidio Heights neighborhood. It's the beginning of the Avenues and close to the old Presidio, which is a former Army base and is now a national park. It's adjacent to the Golden Gate Bridge, so the views can be spectacular. I live in an area of homes that seem like they belong in the suburbs, but within a block are busy streets, high-rise apartments, condos, and great restaurants.

Looking around, he comments, "You're less than ten blocks from my place. This is hardly out of the way."

"I appreciate the ride. Molly will enjoy it. See you in the morning?"

He runs his hands through his hair in what seems like a fit of nervousness. "Hey, can I join you for a walk with your dog?"

Surprised by his request but excited to spend more time with Dillon, I say, "I usually do a run around the park, but I guess we can forgo that today and go for a good walk."

"I don't want to interrupt your exercise, but I miss having a dog, and I think it'll be fun."

"Great. Come on in and you can meet Molly. I should warn you, she's a very active beagle. I'll change out of my dress into something more appropriate for picking up dog poop while you two get acquainted." Molly is a tricolored beagle, barking and baying and demanding all of Dillon's attention, which he graciously lavishes on her with a lot of ear and belly rubs. I run back to my bedroom to change. Grabbing a pair of yoga pants and a Yale Law T-shirt, I walk out and ask, "Ready?"

Disengaging from the dog, he stands. "Let's do it."

"We usually head over to the Presidio. Does that work for you?"

"Of course. I'm here for the time to spend with the dog." As we head out, I let Molly direct where she needs to do her business. After a couple minutes, he turns to me and says, "You have a beautiful place, but I didn't see any signs of a roommate or anyone else. Are you married or seriously involved with anyone?"

I'm surprised by his directness and remember Sara's comment about keeping our personal lives personal. "Me? No. Are you?" I'm not sure why I asked, but if he can ask those questions of me, I can do the same.

"Not really. Never thought it was for me."

"What does 'not really' mean? Sleeping with half a dozen different women but none are serious?"

He blushes and asks, "Why aren't you married? Your brothers can't be scaring them off anymore."

I chuckle. "No, not anymore. I'm single because I live in San Francisco."

"People meet and marry in San Francisco all the time—"

Interrupting, I share, "True. But in my experience, guys struggle with the strong, smart females with an opinion. I figured out a long time ago that it probably isn't in the cards for me."

"I think you're selling yourself short."

"Maybe. I'm not closed off to a relationship. I have a wonderful group of friends, and I don't live waiting for some guy to show up at my door. But if you know of anyone, please feel free to send them my way."

Laughing, he asks, "Okay, what are you looking for?"

"I recognize any guy I'm going to meet is going to come with baggage, so I hope the baggage is carry-on and not needing to be checked."

He has a puzzled look on his face. "What does that mean?"

Smiling big, I explain it to him as if he's in fifth grade. "It means his issues aren't too overwhelming. What about you?"

"I think my requirements are pretty steep. Which, according to my sister, is why I'll be single forever."

I tease, "Fess up. Tell me everything. "

"She needs to be tall. I'm a tall guy, and I don't want to break my back bending over to talk to her all the time while we walk around town. She needs to be comfortable with all walks of life our job brings us in contact with. She needs to not always want a five-star dinner but also be comfortable at a fun hole-in-the-wall burger joint. And with that, she can't be a vegetarian. She needs to eat more than salads. I want someone who has a life outside of me. She needs to understand our work life can overtake our personal life at times. I would love it if she played golf." And then, as if it's an afterthought, he mumbles, "Oh yeah, and she needs to be beautiful and good in bed."

Pushing his shoulder, "Oh, I love how you slipped 'beautiful and good in bed' in there. Can she be trimmed or does she need to be completely bare?"

Laughing hard, he can barely get out "What?"

"Well, if I'm going to try to fix you up with one of my friends and sex is really at the top of your list, what is your preference?"

He's not going to answer my question. Just as well, since I'm not sure what I would do with that information.

As we walk by a strip of small local restaurants, I stop in front of an Italian café and see it's doing a brisk business. "Can I buy you dinner?" I ask.

"No. But since I've hijacked your evening, how about I buy you dinner?"

I'm not used to so much attention from a straight man. During dinner, we talk about so many things. He leans in and listens to my crazy ideas about dating and work-life balance, and I am entirely comfortable with him.

DILLON

*C*MERSON IS HILARIOUS. I can't believe how direct and dry her sense of humor is. She's obviously been hurt, but she isn't bitter like so many women in San Francisco become. We've stopped at a cute little Italian bistro and we both order. I love that she goes for a glass of wine and the lasagna, with a salad as a starter.

"I hope it's okay that I'm ordering a salad as part of my dinner," she teases at what I know is going to become an inside joke for us.

As we settle in to wait for our food with Molly at our feet, I can't help but keep giving the dog pieces of bread. Her big brown eyes are melting my heart. "Okay, now tell me about your perfect guy. Don't be shy."

"I'm not picky. I like my dates taller than me. I'm 5'11" and like to wear heels."

Women always say they're not picky when in reality they really are. I snicker. "I'll determine if you're not picky. Keep going."

"All right already! He must be able to carry on a conversation and not be afraid when my opinion isn't the same as his. He needs to love his mother, but doesn't live at home with her."

I stop her there. "Do you meet many men who still live at home with their mom?

She rolls her eyes and shares, "You'd be surprised."

Laughing, I tell her, "None of my friends live at home. Keep going. You haven't mentioned golf, and we talked about your playing golf at Stanford when you interviewed—which impressed all of us greatly, by the way."

"Well, playing golf is a given. A guy would have to be prepared to lose when we play golf because I won't throw a game for a man's ego."

"What's your handicap?"

"When I was playing every day, and hitting over fifteen hundred practice golf balls a week, I was a minus one. These days, I hit about five hundred golf balls a week in the mornings before work and play at least eighteen holes a week. So I tend to run about a three handicap."

I almost spit out my drink. "A three? You could play on the pro tour."

"That would make my hobby a job. It wouldn't be as fun."

"Well, you'll beat me, but I can take it."

"I didn't say my ego couldn't lose to my boss."

"I'm not your boss, I'm a peer. We're all partners with equal voting rights."

Conspiratorially, she shares, "Then be aware, I give nothing."

"Great. I'll set up a tee time at the Palo Alto Country Club for Saturday morning. You've played there before, haven't you?"

"It's Stanford's home course, so I played at least one round a day there for almost five years. I'm quite familiar with it. Are you sure you want to play there?"

"Of course. The guys and I are all members. It's our home course, too. More of a level playing field."

We talk about random things for a bit longer as we finish our meals. Paying for dinner, I lean in close. "This was fun."

"Yes, it was. You're stuck with me all day tomorrow at Accurate, and Wednesday we have another day together for a different client."

"I think I can handle it."

Walking to her front door, she tells me, "Good night, Dillon."

"Good night, Emerson. I'll bring my running clothes next time so we can take Molly for a run."

She enters her house and turns to wave. "See you tomorrow."

What a fun evening. Very unexpected.

On my short drive home, I call Tiffany and invite her over for the evening. Tiffany is an excellent match for me right now; she's adventurous in bed and doesn't require much of me.

She meets me at my place wearing only a trench coat with stockings and stilettos. I usher her into my home and turn to watch her drop her coat. She doesn't kiss me, just gets on her knees in front of me and undoes my pants, making a small moaning sound as she takes me in her mouth. I'm not completely hard as she starts, but as she licks and sucks the length of my cock, I quickly become as hard as a baseball bat. I love the way she's so keen to make me come. I think about Emerson and wonder what it would be like if she were here doing this to me.

I take a deep breath, enjoying the suction and the pull of her mouth as I grow harder. She pulls me into the kitchen and lies with her back on my kitchen table. Lifting her legs up and wide, she begins circling her clit while watching me. She drives me crazy.

I remove my clothes and place a condom from my pocket on the table while watching her. Getting on my knees, I lick up the sweet taste escaping from the pleasure she's giving herself.

"Please, fuck me!" she begs.

I wish she would let my mouth bring her to her pinnacle, but I stand and grab the condom.

As I open the package, she tells me, "You know, I have an IUD, and I don't fuck anyone else. I'm clean."

I kiss her and keep rolling the condom on my hard and wanting cock. Entering her, I thrust in long, hard strokes. She moans like a porn star. It can be a bit of a turn-off at times, but she's into having sex. I pull and twist at her nipples while pumping hard in and out of her. I love down-and-dirty, carnal sex.

When we're done, she wraps herself in a blanket she finds in my living room, and I grab a pair of sweatpants from my bedroom and a Star Wars T-shirt.

Twirling a strand of her chestnut hair around her finger and avoiding looking at me with her big brown eyes, she tells me, "I would love skin-to-skin contact with you when we have sex."

"I would like that, too, but you know we're not exclusive, and I promise you I use a condom with every woman I sleep with."

She's quiet for a few moments. I can tell she isn't happy with my answer, but I'm in a financial situation where I must be incredibly careful. I don't want her or anyone else attempting to trap me with a baby. I like her, but I'm not sure I want her in my life forever.

Now I would like her to go home, but it would be rude to ask, so we make small talk. Tiffany is a fan of reality TV and talks nonstop about someone's Instagram account. I'm lost, and all I can think about is Emerson.

It's after midnight, so I lean over and tell her, "It's getting late. I need to get up early tomorrow for a few business meetings. As usual, you were incredible. Let's make plans to get together again next week."

Disappointment fills her eyes as she nods. "I can't wait."

When I hand her her coat, she steps in for a deep, wet kiss. I know she wants to stay, but I don't spend the night, and I *always* sleep alone.

EMERSON

WHAT A FUN EVENING. Of the four partners, I'd had the best connection with Dillon when they approached me about buying my company. All the conversations I'd had with the partners were completely professional, but we did talk about my playing for Stanford's golf team as an undergraduate and having gone to Yale for law school.

We spent a lot of time discussing why I chose to leave the actual practice of law and start my business. It seemed to be a way to use my law degree, but in a way, it's more in line with my personal interests. After all, if you're going to spend eighty percent of your day doing something, you might as well enjoy it. Plus, I prefer to keep people out of trouble rather than sitting in a law firm figuring out how to dig people out of the trouble they've found. That drives me crazy.

I like Dillon. He's handsome and, as I figured, he's a player. He's totally my type. He'll be a strong business partner, but if I'm smart, he'll be nothing more than a friend. He's trouble. He most likely isn't a candidate for any of my friends, but who knows?

Calling my best friend, CeCe, I fill her in on my day and the conversation with Dillon.

Scrutinizing my opinion of the conversation, she asks, "Are you sure he isn't hitting on you?"

CeCe was my roommate my freshman year at Stanford, and we've been best friends ever since. She's known me for over fifteen years and knows me better than I know myself. "No. We have a pretty strict non-fraternization clause in our contracts. They feel it could disrupt the balance of power, so it's clear. I see Dillon more like my brother Michael."

She laughs. "You mean trouble."

Michael was consistently in trouble when we were growing up. He's only thirteen months older than I am and he played football at Cal. Just across the bay, we were able to hang out often while in school, and his friends were consistently getting in trouble. CeCe had many drunken nights with Michael and his friends. "Probably, yes."

"Are we getting together this weekend?"

"Let me see what his plans are after golf. Can you hold tight a few days?"

"Sure. I'll put Greer and Hadlee on alert. Maybe dinner and drinks? It would be fun."

"Most likely after my first week at this crazy job, it may be all I can do. Don't let Greer talk you into going to a gay bar for dancing after dinner."

"I promise. Have a good night, and text me tomorrow if you can escape for lunch."

"I'm headed to Mountain View for the day."

"Oookay, fine. No for lunch. Call me, sweetie."

"Promise."

OUR WEDNESDAY goes without much of a hitch. Thursday after work, the partners get together for drinks in the conference room. This is a weekly meeting, and we drink beer and recap the week and any additional work on the horizon.

Dillon shares the research teams finding on two more start-ups that look interesting. As we pour through the P&Ls and other parts of their financial status, I watch the group dynamics. Everyone offers their opinions in their areas of expertise. When they come to me, I'm careful when I share my concerns. Mason drills down, asking more in-depth questions, and in the end, we agree to not invest in the company.

AS I LIE IN BED REPLAYING MY WEEK, the partners meeting this afternoon in particular, I think of how much power I have. The company would've invested about five million dollars for our first round, and we considered a total of over fifteen million. I shared that I'm concerned about the chief financial officer not really understanding basic accounting principles. We could've required they hire someone else, which is what I'm advocating, but Mason felt that they should've figured it out on their own. This power scares me a little bit.

DILLON

I MENTIONED to Mason that I'm going to play a round of golf with Emerson on Saturday, and now Mason and Cameron have plans to join us and make it a foursome. The three of us became members of the Palo Alto Country Club when we were in our mid-twenties with too much money on our hands, and as junior members, it wasn't as expensive.

The Palo Alto Country Club can be a who's who of Silicon Valley, but it's really a beautiful green oasis close to Stanford. It has rolling greens with more sand traps than I would like and certainly some challenging water hazards. What really makes the course unique are the spectacular views of the Bay Area. The head golf pro has this uncanny knack of moving the pins on each hole regularly, which adds to the complexity. This is the home course to four PGA and LPGA tour professionals.

The guys are bringing a lot of bravado to Saturday morning. We're decent players, but we're definitely weekend hackers. I don't know why they think they have a chance in hell to beat Emerson. I'm sure she's still a great player, and I think she'll take this as a bit of hazing and not be too intimidated by us. We also agree to have Sara and some of our friends meet us afterward for drinks and fun at the club bar.

WE MEET FOR A 10:30 A.M. TEE TIME and find Emerson dressed in a white golf skirt with a blue geometric pattern and a matching blue shirt. She's striking with her long tan legs that seem to go on forever. She's chatting with the head pro as I approach.

"I've missed you, too, Tom," I hear her tell him.

"Hopefully we'll see more of you in the coming months and years."

"Well I'm only here as a guest, but I sure do miss this course. How are the greens running today?"

"I'd say they're fast. We're soaking the greens at night, but the hot weather is drying out the greens by this time of day."

"Anything else I should know before I let these guys beat me?"

Making my presence known, I interject, "You better not play below your abilities. We're all here to watch you play."

Tom shares with me, "You know she qualified for the women's pro tour every year she was at Stanford. Two of her teammates, who weren't half as good, have gone on to play pro and are making a decent living."

Emerson turns to me. "Tom here has always been the president of my fan club. I was never as good as Tina Martin or Jenny Wolf."

"Don't let her fool you. Those two girls may be in the top twenty in the world, but she's better. You'll see."

We're in so much trouble. Please don't embarrass us too much.

We meet the guys at the first tee with our golf carts. I set this up, so I'm riding with Emerson. I've loaded up an ice chest of Bloody Marys and beer chasers. The three of us drive our first shots off to the first hole's middle tee, some of us with less-than-stellar first hits. We're expecting Emerson to move to the front tees, but she chooses the back instead.

Mason looks at me and seems stunned. Cameron mutters, "She's going to kill us today, isn't she?"

We all nod and Mason says, "Yep."

She has the most brilliant drive, and even with the extra ten yards she added by using the back tee, she outpaces our first shots by another ten yards. We all look at each other and know we're going to get handed our lunch today.

Mason says, "This is going to be fun watching her play, and I probably won't mind if she beats me."

We all nod in agreement.

In the cart, Emerson asks, "Was that showing off?"

I laugh and tell her, "Not in the least. We're all prepared to get spanked today, and we'll enjoy watching you do it. But I should warn you, you're going to be pulled into every tournament we get invited to—particularly when we play best ball tourneys."

"I'll manage."

The round of golf lasted almost four hours. Emerson didn't offer any advice unless it was solicited, always the consummate professional as she killed us all. She beat me by nearly eight strokes and Cameron by at least one stroke every hole.

Emerson forced each of us to pony up five hundred dollars we'd each secretly bet before the start of the first hole. I laughed so hard my sides hurt as we began to drag ourselves to the club bar.

"Emerson, you're truly a fantastic player. Real treat to watch you play. I'm glad you're on our team," Mason says.

Everyone laughs as we put our gear away in our club lockers and meet Sara and a few friends at the bar in the clubhouse. I've invited an old friend of mine from college to join us. "Adam, this is Emerson. Emerson, Adam."

"Nice to meet you," they both say in unison.

Sara is watching all the attention Emerson is getting and seems unhappy. Emerson notices too and asks, "Sara, do you play golf?"

Holding her purse tight to her side, Sara blushes, apparently embarrassed. "No. Not very well."

Emerson teases, "That sounds like a yes."

"I play about four times a year. I'm nowhere near as good as you or the guys though. My best sport is being a professional spectator."

"Well, I hope you'll join us next time. Dillon here can ride by himself and we girls can enjoy time together."

Sara naturally relaxes at the idea of being included. "I'd love to."

We spend better than two hours just hanging out and chatting it up. Sara gets a text and politely excuses herself. I suspect she has a date with a hot new beau, and I'm thrilled Sara's seeing someone. She's a great girl and deserves a guy who adores her.

I asked Adam to be at the bar to meet Emerson. As one of my good friends, I remember Adam talking about her when we were in school and thought they might like one another. Now that

I've seen them together, however, I'm not sure I like the idea of them going out.

Adam leans over and asks Emerson if she'd like to go to dinner sometime. She blushes as she agrees and gives him her phone number. For some reason, it bothers me.

I like her friend CeCe. She looks familiar, but I can't place from where exactly. Like Emerson, she's tall with an hourglass figure—extremely easy on the eyes. A vivacious brunette, she comfortably fits in with our crew and seems to be able to take as much as she can dish out. Mason is completely taken by her, though he's seeing someone and would never stray. Maybe if he spends more time with her in these kinds of settings, he'll find that Grace, his current girlfriend, isn't such a good match for him.

The sun is getting low, and Emerson makes a polite excuse for her and CeCe to head home. Mason asks, "CeCe, have you been here all morning?"

"Oh goodness no. I took a Lyft down knowing I could catch a ride with Em back into The City."

Awkwardly, Mason says, "Well, I hope we'll see you again."

With a bright smile, she gives him a hug. "I hope so, too."

The valets help Emerson load her car with her clubs, and she talks to a few of the staff who remember her from her Stanford days. That was over fifteen years ago, which speaks volumes to how she's always been with people. I watch as CeCe sits next to her in her car and wave as they drive back into The City.

On my drive home, I call Elizabeth and ask her out for a last-minute dinner. She agrees, and I tell her I'll pick her up at eight o'clock at the door of her building. I then call and make reservations at the newest hot restaurant.

I'm waiting outside Elizabeth's building. It's after eight, and she's late. She's recently out of grad school in Chicago, cute and decent in bed. She works for Clorox and is always eager to please; however, she's never on time, which drives me crazy.

As we walk into the restaurant, the manager is there waiting for us and we're quickly shown our seat. As I look across the busy restaurant, I'm shocked when I see Emerson and CeCe with two other women. I tell Elizabeth that I'll be right back and I walk over.

I open my arms wide as I approach the table. "Hey, girls!"

CeCe jumps up and gives me a big hug, then introduces me to the girls I don't know. "Ladies, this is Dillon Healy, Emerson's yummy new business partner. Dillon, this is Hadlee Fisher and Greer Ford."

CeCe moved from golf attire to a striking sleeveless fringed black cocktail dress. It's short and shows off her well-toned arms, her long legs accentuated with a strappy high-heeled sandal. CeCe's chestnut hair is straight down her back, and her big brown eyes are emphasized by smoky makeup.

Hadlee could easily pass for a sister to Kate Beckinsale with dark brown hair and stunning sapphire-blue eyes. Her dark floral print dress hugs and highlights every delicious curve, and the blue in the floral really make her eyes pop.

Greer has a more traditional voluptuous figure, very generous and luscious. The long-sleeved lacy sheath dress in a beautiful medium brown tone highlights her auburn-colored hair quite nicely.

Emerson is a sight to behold with her blonde hair piled high on her head, ringlets cascading down strategically around her face. Her embroidered cap sleeve sheath cocktail dress hits above her beautiful knees. At first, I think her dress strategically covers all the good parts, but then I realize it has a skintone slip underneath. It's very sexy. Those strappy sandals are quickly becoming my favorite, and her makeup is subtle. I easily imagine her pink lips sucking my cock.

All four women are gorgeous. Even the gay men in the restaurant are clearly mesmerized by the quartet. I tell them I'm with a friend and ask if they'd like to make it a table of six. We all agree, and I grab the hostess. She tries to tell me they're unable to accommodate my request, but then I do the one thing I hate and ask her to find the manager. She walks off in a huff, he comes over, and we have a bigger table.

I introduce Elizabeth to everyone, and she's obviously disappointed that she no longer has my individual attention. The women are gracious and friendly, and she gets over her disappointment quickly.

"Dillon, I hope you're treating our Emerson well at SHN," Greer asks.

Emerson is quick to interject, "They're doing fine."

"Dillon, you up for some dancing in the Castro tonight?" Hadlee questions me.

I laugh and tell her, "You might be able to talk me into it."

She squeals in delight, clapping her hands in front of her like a young child. Turning to Emerson, she says, "Emerson, you're the only one who seems to be uninterested."

"Why go to a gay bar?" Emerson asks. "There isn't anything I have that interests them. Most of the time, it seems as if we're taking up valuable space from the hordes of men who might be potential dates for the night."

Confused, Elizabeth asks the girls, "You like to hang out in gay bars?"

"Honey, it's the best entertainment in town, and the dancing is a blast," CeCe tells her.

We order a nice dinner and have a fun night, though we're loud and probably a little rowdier than we should be. It's almost midnight before we know it, and I wave down the waiter and ask for the check. Everyone reaches for their wallets except Elizabeth. I did ask her out, so I'm not surprised, just maybe a bit disappointed. I tell everyone, "Put your wallets away. I've got this," and when the waiter arrives, I hand him my Black American Express card.

As we all leave the restaurant, Emerson gives everyone—including Elizabeth and me—a deep embrace, then asks the valet to call her a cab. I tell her I'll give her a ride home, but I quickly realize I drove my Porsche and there's no place for Elizabeth if I take Emerson.

"Don't worry about me. I can take a cab home," Emerson assures me.

CeCe has a limo on call, which drives up to pick them up. The girls are gracious and ask if we want to head into the Castro with them. We politely decline and send the three girls on their way. Emerson's cab pulls up and she waves goodbye as she climbs into her ride home.

As they drive off, Elizabeth cuddles in and says, "We're finally alone."

It dawns on me that I'm not interested in being alone with her. As my car arrives and she sits in the passenger seat, her hand immediately wanders to my crotch and she strokes me. I'm not feeling anything for her or what she's doing; I can't even get hard. I turn to her and say, "Can we try another night? I'm tired and have an early morning tomorrow."

"Sure," she pouts.

I drop her at her place and head home, unable to get Emerson out of my mind. I like her friends. They're apparently pretty tight, and she made sure to spotlight each of the girls for me in such a way that it wouldn't make Elizabeth jealous. It was the most fun I've had out in a long time.

Emerson has entered my life with all kinds of surprises.

EMERSON

THE DRIVE HOME in the taxi is taking much longer than I would have liked, but it gives me time to reflect on the evening. Elizabeth is attractive, and much younger than I expected. Cute girl. She wasn't too thrilled about being part of our harem, but hopefully she had an excellent time.

I'm not sure I wanted Hadlee to meet Dillon. I know she'll ask me if she can get his number and ask him out, which will make work a bit embarrassing. I'll have to tell him about the possibility and let him make the call. I'm not going to get in the middle.

When I get home, I quickly change and take Molly out for a short walk. She's tired, too, so she does her business quickly and we're soon home cuddling in bed. I continue to replay the evening in my mind. It was a lot of fun, but I'm glad to have Molly to come home to every night. She adores me and is always excited to see me. I lie here wondering how nice it would be to have Dillon here in my bed to cuddle up with as I slowly drift off to sleep.

MOLLY AND I wake early and head out for a good run. I enjoy the exercise. The soft sounds of birds chirping in the trees above me always cause my heart to flutter in my chest. They help to remind me that San Francisco isn't just a concrete jungle. We run shy of five miles around the Presidio, and she's exhausted by the time we get home. As I run, I always work out my stress of the day and any challenges I'm facing. Honestly, I hate to work out, but I like to eat, so I don't have much choice.

Arriving home, I see a text from Dillon.

Dillon Healy: You interested in meeting for breakfast?

Emerson Winthrop: Sure. I just got back from a run. I need to shower. What time were you thinking?

Dillon Healy: I can come by and pick you up when you're ready.

Emerson Winthrop: OK. 30 minutes.

Dillon Healy: You're fast. See you then.

Surprised to see the voice mail icon on my phone, I quickly check it and am stunned to hear Adam's voice. I missed his call at some point yesterday. He wanted to meet up last night. Too late. Even if he'd caught me, I don't go out last minute. Oh well.

I quickly grab a shower and dress casually. Just as I finish up, Dillon rings the bell.

"Hi. Come on in. I'm ready, just need to get Molly settled before I go."

"Hey. No worries." Looking around, he watches me as I tempt Molly into her crate. "I've never known a woman who could get ready so fast.

"Growing up in a family of five kids, who all share one bathroom, you learn to be quick."

"One bathroom for the five of you? That's tight." He removes a bone from his pocket, and Molly is smitten. She sits at his feet in a begging position and can't take her eyes off his hand with the bone.

Molly frustratingly keeps running over to Dillon for belly and ear rubs instead of going into her crate. "You do know she may want to go live with you if you continue to spoil her."

"That's what I'm counting on. So... the bathroom?

"My parents restored old homes as a hobby. It was fun, but it often meant we lived in tight quarters. I usually got my own room as the only girl." Changing subjects, I ask, "How did it go last night with Elizabeth? She couldn't have been too thrilled to share you with four other women."

"We're just friends."

I stop and turn to him. "Dillon, I don't think she thinks of you as a friend."

Shrugging, he says, "Well, maybe not, but I think of Elizabeth as only a friend. And I dropped her off at her place last night."

"She must have been disappointed."

He shrugs like he doesn't care what Elizabeth wants.

Definitely a player.

DILLON

$\mathcal{I}$ COULDN'T GET Emerson out of my mind last night. Once I thought it was a reputable hour, I texted her for breakfast. I could come up with a work excuse if I needed to, but I like hanging out with her. I'm delighted when she texts me back that she's up for joining me. It shouldn't have surprised me that she had already gone for a good run this morning. From hitting golf balls before work and a few other things she's said, I figured she was a morning person.

We head to a spot in my neighborhood for breakfast. It's still early for the Sunday crowd, so we get a decent table. We both order coffee and enjoy sitting and reading the *San Francisco Chronicle*. It's comfortable. When the bill arrives, she insists on paying. What a welcome change from most of the women in my life.

"We aren't dating. I can pay my own way. You know what I make."

"I do, but you do know I make more than you do."

"So? You take more risk than I do."

"Eventually you'll do the same. But if it's important to you,

you may buy breakfast." I love the look of triumph she has when she gets her way. Makes me wonder what faces she makes when she comes. I would love to find out.

As we walk out together, I ask, "Would you be interested in joining me for a walk through the farmer's market?"

"Sounds perfect." It's down the street, so we walk over.

We wander the thirty white tent–covered stalls filled with beautiful fresh produce from local farms, fresh seafood caught from off the northern California coast, stunning colorful bouquets of flowers matching every color in a big box of crayons, fragrant smells of freshly baked bread, and artists and craftsmen selling their wares. We enjoy everything the market has to offer, each picking up a few items.

Emerson buys all sorts of salad fixings and explains with all the eating out and catering at the office, she's going to eat more salads. "You can't hold it against me. You guys are trying to fatten all the girls up." I also love that she buys herself an enormous bouquet of daisies. Nothing ornate but a simple happy flower. "They're my favorite," she shares with a giant smile.

As we walk, we talk a little about work and what our week is going to look like. I'm going into the office this afternoon, and Emerson plans on working from her couch at home with Molly at her feet.

EMERSON

$\mathcal{J}$T WAS A BEAUTIFUL morning with Dillon. It's going to be hard for me not to fall for him. He's my type—confident, athletic, smart, and he's incredibly good-looking. Of course, the no-fraternization clause in our contracts is pretty strict, so I'm not about to have them claw back over half of the money they paid me for my company because of my hormones. I can keep my distance.

And may I remind myself, he's a player. He has an extensive list of girls he screws. Not a smart move to join that club.

He drops me at home so he can go into the office. As he drives away, I feel a bit of emptiness, though I do take comfort in knowing I'll see him in the morning.

Now I have to tackle this call from Adam. I start with a call to CeCe to get her thoughts first.

She answers the phone sounding half-conscious. "Are you awake yet?"

"Of course. I've even had breakfast and went to the farmer's market with a friend." I'm playing tug-o-war with Molly and stop.

No longer sounding like I've woken her, CeCe is alert and acutely aware that I'm a bit cagey. "Really? What friend?"

"No one worth talking about...yet."

I settle on my couch, and Molly crawls into my lap and looks at me with her big brown eyes begging for attention. I subconsciously stroke her soft fur. "I got a call from Dillon's friend Adam yesterday. I didn't pick it up until this morning. Can you believe he asked me out for last night?"

"Really? Is Adam the guy you had breakfast and 'wandered the farmer's market' with?"

I giggle. "Nope. Someone totally different."

"Okay, well, have you called Adam back yet?"

"No. I thought you could help me psych myself up for it." Disappointed at the reality of single life in San Francisco, I ask, "Could this be what we girls are doing wrong?"

"Being too available?"

"Yes. Or is this city getting so bad that guys think we'll jump with two hours' notice?"

CeCe's tone is firm. "Absolutely not. We're not desperate sluts."

"No. I'm presently a nun, so I'm definitely not a slut."

"Hon, it's only drinks and maybe dinner. Not sex. Go have a fun night and keep it friendly."

"I know. But honestly, I'm not super excited about Adam. He's tight with Dillon, and when this goes sideways—which it will—I don't want it to affect my relationship with Dillon." I give a big sigh. "Okay, fine, I can make it work."

"Let me know how it goes."

I call him back and he flippantly asks me out for tonight. I patiently explain that I don't actually go out on school nights and he's surprised. His attitude changes a bit after that, as if he's used to getting his own way. We talk a bit more and make tentative plans to meet next Saturday.

It won't surprise me if he cancels because something better came along. Wouldn't that be a relief!

I call CeCe back and share the odd conversation. We're both puzzled by it but don't dwell on it. She does circle back to the Dillon conversation. I share with her that I spent the morning with him, and my surprise that he didn't spend last night with Elizabeth.

CeCe reminds me, "It doesn't mean he didn't have sex with her."

"I know, but he did say he dropped her at home after he left the restaurant."

"Honey, Dillon's very sweet on you."

"I don't know about that. It's always brotherly with him."

"He didn't go home and sleep with Elizabeth—it's a huge sign."

Wanting to get off the subject, I tell her, "I'm headed down to Hillsboro to have dinner with my parents tonight. Any interest in joining me? They'd love to see you."

"So tempting but no. I have work to get done. Rain check?"

"Rain check. Talk to you later this week."

During our Monday partners meeting, we go over proposals and are surprised to find we've recently lost two potential investments. Mason shares with me that we've never lost any potential investments in almost five years, which explains why everyone is shocked and the disappointment is evident.

"How is this possible?" asks Mason.

"Good question. I wanted those start-ups in our portfolio, and I've worked the numbers several times. They were great investments, but not for more than what we were offering. Who got them?" Dillon asks.

Sara shares, "I understand it was Perkins Klein. They offered ten percent more money and a smaller equity percentage. How is it good business for them?"

Cameron thoughtfully adds, "They have solid technology, but I don't think ten percent more is worth it for less than twenty percent equity. This may just be an opportunity for Perkins Klein to pad their portfolio."

We discuss it a bit longer to manage our shock, then eventually all agree with Cameron's assessment and go back to our work.

⁂

It was a crazy week. My team added six new clients to manage, and I developed an implementation team covering all the operations. We go into each client company and work with their existing teams, providing backup and support. In rare cases, they may be outsourcing their work, and we help to evaluate if work should be transitioned to my team, we should hire someone internally for them, or have everything remain as it is.

Because we're investors and our goal is to either sell to larger companies or go public, we're continuously evaluating. Our clients know we have a team looking at the weaknesses they'll face that can affect the ability to sell or go public.

Mason is the best at explaining to entrepreneurs that they will always be the founder, but sometimes their strength is seeing the vision of their technology and not the vision of their company.

My team's heaviest dedication is typically in recruiting, and I'm proud to say I have the best recruiters in the Bay Area. I'm lucky to have my team; they work hard and care about the employees while watching the bottom line.

As the week progresses, I'm so busy that I forget I have a tentative date with Adam.

He calls me Friday morning to confirm, and we agree on a time and place to meet the next night. I'm actually surprised he hasn't found someone more apt to sleep with him and canceled our dinner. I must admit, I'm not looking forward to going out with him, disappointed in myself that I agreed to go on this date. I want the excuse to not go, but nothing is coming to mind that won't get back to Dillon.

Saturday morning, Dillon and I play a round of golf at his club, where he puts me through my paces. We get along well and often bicker like siblings.

I've been debating telling Dillon about Adam, because I like Dillon and I learned a long time ago that guys won't date a girl if she's gone out with one of their friends. I know I don't want to date Dillon, but what we're building is really important to me and I don't want to ruin it.

As we hit the sixteenth hole, I finally find the courage, though I wait until he's ready to putt. We do have a brother-sister relationship, and if I can use a perceived weakness, I'm going to exploit it.

"I have a date with Adam tonight."

He looks up from his putt. "Really? That was fast." He follows through on his stroke and still makes the putt.

Drat. Does nothing distract him?

"He asked me out last Saturday for Saturday night. You boys are getting a little too comfortable being single and straight in San Francisco."

With a deep laugh, he says, "We probably are. I'm guilty of that all the time. I can't count on my schedule going as planned. What are you guys doing tonight?"

I can feel the relationship we've built cooling. This isn't what I want. Trying to be nonchalant and uncaring, I tell him, "We're meeting for drinks at the Redwood Room in The Clift Hotel and then dinner at Farallon in Union Square."

Stiffly, he says, "A fun vibe at the Redwood Room and good seafood at Farallon."

"Farallon is a favorite of mine."

DILLON

HEARING EMERSON HAS A DATE with Adam bothers me more than it should. We're only friends, of course, and Adam's a good guy. I introduced them, after all, though mostly because when we were in school, he once made a comment about her and I thought he would enjoy meeting her.

After our round of golf, we grab a beer in the clubhouse. I know this sounds strange, but I feel more at ease with Emerson than I do with anyone else. She isn't like many of the women I know. Emerson has much more confidence. She isn't scared to share her opinion if it's different than mine, and I like that she has a lot of opinions. She doesn't overwhelm you with them, but she does manage to share, a quality I find most intriguing.

As I drive home, I realize I don't have any plans and don't want to be alone tonight; I guess I thought I would be spending the day and evening with Emerson and never made plans.

I decide I haven't seen Bethany, my mortgage broker, in a while. She's always up for a good time. I call her from my car, and she answers in a seductive and breathless voice. "Hey there, handsome."

"Hey. You up for getting together for dinner and... whatever tonight?"

"You know I'm always up for 'whatever' with you. I'll change my plans. What time are you thinking?"

I don't want to be anywhere near where Adam and Emerson are meeting up tonight. I'm thinking going into the Mission district will guarantee I won't see the couple. "How about I meet you at Foreign Cinema about eight?"

"See you then, sweetheart."

Bethany will be a good distraction from Emerson's date tonight.

EMERSON

I'M DREADING THE DATE but drag myself through getting ready in black palazzo pants with a high-necked pink cashmere sweater, a short pearl necklace, matching pearl stud earrings, and my favorite Jimmy Choo sandals. I look good and yet a little conservative, perfect considering I don't want to put off any signals that say I want to get laid tonight.

We meet at The Clift Hotel, off Union Square and a block from Farallon. The Clift has this swanky lounge called the Redwood Room, with a vast selection of bourbons that Adam is looking for. I'm a scotch girl, but I can enjoy a glass of bourbon on occasion.

Adam arrives and looks quite handsome in black pants and coat with a black dress shirt. I'm the envy of many of the women in the bar looking for a companion for the evening. He knows he looks good, and he's turning on the charm. He grazes my temple as he pushes the hair out of my face. His hands wander, but I never feel uncomfortable.

He holds my hand as we walk over to Farallon, but I don't feel any chemistry with Adam. He's handsome and funny, but his touch doesn't send any jolts to my core, and I have no desire to kiss him.

Farallon is my favorite seafood restaurant in San Francisco. As you walk in, a Dale Chuilly–inspired hand-blown glass sculpture of jellyfish fills the ceiling, giving you the feeling of being underwater. They are famous for their raw oyster bar, but I don't want to provide Adam with any ideas, so I order the scallops with a salad starter. He orders the most expensive thing on the menu—steak and lobster. I figure he's trying to impress me.

The conversation between us is easy, starting with where we're from. Adam grew up in Southern California with three sisters and had a similar upbringing as me with my brothers, as his sisters wouldn't let girls near him. Sharing sibling stories is fun, though it seems his sisters were much harder than my brothers.

He met Dillon playing football while at Stanford. He mentions we met once at Stanford, but I don't remember. I admit, "I was overwhelmed at school. Playing golf was competitive, and I couldn't afford to lose my scholarship. Was I a bitch when we met?"

He laughs. "No, not at all. You were sweet and a bit shy."

"Oh, that's good. I was awkward at that point. Because of my brothers, boys never looked at me twice growing up. Suddenly they were interested, and I was socially immature, so I often didn't know how to respond but to be every guy's friend."

"You were the girl who moves the guy into the 'friend zone,'" he says in a knowing tone.

"Guilty as charged. But then I never knew how to move them out. So, tell me about what you've done since school."

I hear some bitterness as he shares the struggles of finding the right start-up that will make it big.

I reach across the table and touch his hand. "Most people aren't as lucky as Dillon to hit it big. Don't measure your success against his luck."

"That's what I tell myself. I know Dillon's a great guy, and we enjoy the occasional pickup basketball game." Changing subjects, he asks, "Are you enjoying yourself tonight? Do you want to go back to the Redwood Room at The Clift for a last drink before we call it a night?"

"Sure. I have a full workday tomorrow, but I can manage one more drink."

We walk the two blocks and he's a complete gentleman, offering me his coat. The fog has rolled in and the temperature seems to drop significantly.

We walk into the crowded Redwood Room lounge, the golden glow cast by the Art Deco pendant lamps hung from the ceiling making it dark and mysterious. Behind the bar, seven glass shelves covered in exotic liquors add to the ambiance of a fashionable place to be seen. It's a combination of tourists, locals, MILFs, and I'm sure a few who are barely eighteen. More women than men, but that's par for a straight bar in San Francisco.

Adam grabs a spot at one of the tables, the high-back red leather banquette offering a level of privacy and romance. We watch the people around us and are surprised when we see an eighties rock star and heartthrob.

"I wonder if he's here to play a show?" I ask.

"I think I read he's in a local musical preparing to go to Broadway. Look at the girls throwing themselves at him." We laugh and watch as a beautiful Asian woman hands him something. Adam leans in and whispers, "Did she just give him her panties?"

In shock, I nod. "I think she did."

"Lucky guy," Adams says with a lot of envy.

The bartender takes our order, and I excuse myself and head to the ladies' room. And that's the last thing I remember.

As I WAKE FROM A HAZE-FILLED SLEEP, I'm not sure where I am. All I know is I'm in a strange bed, I'm naked, and I hurt all over.

Trying to get my bearings, I figure out I'm in a hotel room, and I think it's Sunday morning. I have a splitting headache.

"Oh, you're awake. Good morning, sunshine." Adam leans over and kisses me.

I'm shocked, scared, and bewildered. "Wh-wh-where are we?"

"In a room at The Clift."

Trying to keep the panic at bay, I search my memory for what happened after going to the bathroom. "How did I get here?"

"You begged me to get a room and fuck you."

I'm appalled that I would *ever* beg Adam for anything like that. "What? That can't be possible."

He runs his finger up my arm. "Emerson, you're a fantastic lay. Last night you were truly amazing. Probably the best I've ever had."

I slowly sit up and look around the room. The light is too bright, and my head feels like someone is using a jackhammer inside my skull. I have no memory of last night, though I can taste semen in my throat, and from the feel of it, I have no doubt we had anal and vaginal sex. My brain isn't working fast enough. The panic is beginning to rise.

"I've got to get home." He kisses me again and I want to vomit. "Let's do this again."

I am utterly speechless. I don't remember anything past going to the bathroom at the bar. I'm having a vision of myself being fucked from behind in the mirror across from the bed, but the memories are only fragments—something that seems more like short vignettes or photos. My stomach falls as I realize Adam put something in my drink and I've been date-raped.

My lack of memory of the night has me terrified as I lie in the bed with my head pounding. I'm thirsty but every limb hurts, and I can't summon the energy to get a glass of water. It takes time, but I curl into a fetal position in the bed and begin to weep, which eventually turns into a deep cry. I'm mad at myself for doing the one thing every single girl is taught never to do.

Never leave your drink unattended. I was so stupid! I brought this on myself.

He's a good friend of Dillon's, and I don't want to get the police involved. I crawl into the shower and sit there trying to wash away the dirty feeling I have of Adam touching me and fucking me.

Shit! I don't even know if we used a condom.

The realization brings a real level of panic and I crawl out of the shower.

Housekeeping is knocking, and I'm told checkout is in less than an hour. I cry harder, then do the only thing I can think to do: I call my best friend. CeCe doesn't answer, but I leave her a message, crying my way through it. "I'm at The Clift Hotel, and I don't know what to do. I have no memory of last night. I think he slipped something in my drink. I'm getting a cab and heading home." Through the string of tears, I can barely get out, "Call me."

I search for what seems like forever for my panties but I can't find them. I put my pants and sweater set on from the night before and pull my hair into a wet ponytail. My hands are shaking, and I keep seeing a reflection in the mirror next to the bed of Adam fucking me from behind.

What the fuck did Adam do with my panties? Fuck it! I need to get home and away from here.

As I prepare to walk out the door, CeCe calls. "I'm on my way. I should be there in five minutes. I'll meet you out front. We're going to the police station and reporting the son of a bitch."

I feel so much comfort in knowing CeCe is on her way and can help me sort through this. I hurt everywhere, and I wish I had a toothbrush; I can still taste his cum in my mouth. I find the bank of elevators and take one down, thankfully alone.

The doorman holds the door for me as I exit to Geary Street and wishes me a good day. The sky is gray, and the fog leaving a light mist seems incredibly oppressive. I'm struggling to keep it together when I see CeCe come to a screeching halt in her red convertible Mercedes, jump out, and come rushing up to me.

I start crying as I walk into her arms for a comforting hug.

"What the fuck happened?"

"I don't know. I honestly don't know."

"What do you mean you don't know?"

"I broke rule one of the single girl codes. I ordered a drink, went to the bathroom and that is the last thing I remember. I have snippets of memories, but nothing concrete."

Bringing me in for a tighter embrace, CeCe is crying, too. "I'm sorry."

"It's my fault. I'm mad at myself."

"You trusted Dillon's friend. I probably would have, too, honey. We need to get you to the hospital, or at the very least the police station, report the incident, and get a rape kit done."

"No! He's Dillon's friend, and I don't want anyone at the office to know."

"Are you sure? I really think we need to do this in case you change your mind later."

"No. I've already showered and washed away any evidence. I just want to go home."

"Okay, let's get you home and changed."

CeCe drops me at my place and helps me into a pair of sweatpants and a hoodie. "Are you sure I can't convince you to file a police report?"

There is a silence to my soul; the weight I carry is overwhelming. The blame I place is squarely at my feet. The time I can't account for puts a chill in my blood. A coldness brings my brain to a standstill. Part of it is anger, and part of it is pain. I can endure what Adam has done to me, but I can't sleep through night after night without seeing the visions and knowing something went terribly wrong. It's no one's fault but my own, and for that, I have to learn to live with my colossal mistake. "No. I can't take any more humiliation."

She hugs me. "Honey, you can't blame yourself. He drugged you. This wasn't your fault."

Trying not to cry again, all I can do is nod.

"I'm going to sit with you as long as you need me to."

"I love you, but I want to be alone. Do you mind?"

"Of course not. You know I'll be here if you need me."

Reluctantly, CeCe leaves. Once she does, I curl up with Molly on my couch and cry, not only because of the violation but because the personal security I've always had is gone. I know a run would do me good, but I can't even bring myself to go out.

CeCe calls and checks on me, and I assure her I'm fine, even though I'm not.

IN THE DAYS SINCE MY DATE WITH ADAM, insomnia is the companion that won't quit. Time has taken on a different form, more plentiful than it ever has been. The quiet moments cause me to relive all I did wrong, to search for the missing pieces in my memory. He's a friend of my friend. In all these wakeful hours, a shock lingers that I suppress. I can't quite let it surface because every time it comes close, my nightmare solidifies, causing all hope to fade and the sick feeling to return to my guts.

DILLON

$\mathcal{S}$OMETHING IS OFF with Emerson. She isn't her typical happy and playful self, and she's spent the last two months working fifteen-hour days seven days a week. Each time I've asked her to do something with me outside of work, she politely brushes me off.

The circles under her eyes are dark, and her clothes are hanging on her because she's lost too much weight.

She doesn't seem to want to talk to me, so I do the only thing I can: I make an appointment with her for lunch under the guise of discussing a prospective client.

As we sit down at the restaurant, I place a napkin on my lap and begin to peruse the menu. The waiter pours us glasses of water, and I take in our surroundings. I'm not sure I know where to start. I can tell she's nervous as she fingers the sides of the menu. I debate how to ask what's bothering her, so I begin with a softball question. "How are things going at the firm?"

She looks up from the menu, glances around nervously, and says, "Fine."

Fine? I pull out all my boyish charms, move my head to the side, and ask with a crooked smile, "Fine?"

With a half smile, she says, "Yes, fine."

She clearly doesn't want to tell me what's bothering her. Because she doesn't share the possibility that one of our clients or someone from the staff has screwed up, I deduce that it's personal. We've always had a strong connection, so I attempt to take a different approach. "What's wrong? You're working yourself to the bone. Please tell me. Is the work too much? Are you regretting the sale?"

"The work is fine. Really." She smiles once more, but it doesn't reach her eyes.

The waiter returns and takes our order, and we make conversation about each of the clients she's working with. I'm impressed with the talent and recruiting plans she and her team are creating for our clients.

The conversation is good, but Emerson is keeping it professional and distant with me. Her laugh is stilted, and the sound drives a stake through my heart. When our food arrives, I watch her push the salad she ordered around her plate and maybe take two bites. I rib her about eating salad, but she only smiles half-heartedly. She isn't eating, and she isn't admitting anything, but she also won't invite me into what's bothering her.

I decide to take a different tactic.

"Hey, how are things going with Adam? Did you two ever get your date?"

Her beautiful blue eyes cloud over, and what seems like a look of panic crosses through them, but she only tells me "It didn't work out."

There is something there, I can tell. I'm hopeful that I can get Emerson to open up, so I push hard for her to meet me for a round of golf on Saturday.

She's reluctant to go, but I tease her and she eventually gives in after I promise it'll only be the two of us. I'm excited to spend more time with her, so of course it's fine with me.

After we return to the office, I call and get us a tee time. Sending her an invite through our office calendar function, I also let her know I can stop by and pick her up Saturday morning.

I spend the afternoon thinking about our conversation, about how Emerson's entire demeanor changed when I asked about Adam. I figure it must have something to do with him. Once I get home, I call him, hoping to gain a little insight. After working our way through the gossip of some mutual friends, I ask him, "Hey, how did it go with Emerson?"

After a short pause, his voice becomes stilted. "Emerson? Who's Emerson?"

Puzzled by his response, I explain, "She's the woman I work with. You met her and mooned over her in college, and then I introduced you when we all hung out at the club, remember?"

"Oh yeah. Her. We went out months ago. I hardly remember that night. Must not have been fun," he tells me, still sounding wooden.

My Spidey Sense is tingling. Something isn't adding up, and I'm determined to get to the bottom of what happened between the two of them.

IT'S 2:00 A.M. SATURDAY MORNING, and I'm watching *Sports Center* and relaxing, too excited about seeing Emerson to sleep.

My phone pings, telling me I have a text message. It's Emerson.

Sorry, not feeling well. Won't be able to make golf today.

I text her back immediately. Hey. I'm up, can I stop by Lucca's and pick you up some soup? Or the drugstore for some meds?

She doesn't respond.

Something is definitely not right. She's avoiding me, and I want to know why. It's time to confront her.

As soon as it's light, I run by the drugstore and get cold and flu medicine, then stop and buy a hot tea before driving over to see Emerson. All of the curtains are pulled close and I can't see in. I can hear the television but can't make out what show is playing. I knock on the door and Molly barks.

I knock again and call out, "Emerson? It's me, Dillon." I rest my forehead on the door and listen, but don't hear anything. "Please open up. I'm worried about you." She still doesn't answer. I'm getting nervous that she may have passed out on the floor or is too injured to open the door. I hear a click but I can't be sure. I try the doorknob and it's unlocked.

When I walk in, Molly greets me with her tail wagging and her tongue full of dog kisses. I bend down and give her lots of attention, at the same time noticing Emerson's house smells musty and stale. As my eyes adjust to the darkness, I see her curled up on the couch. "Hey, sweetie. Are you feeling okay?"

She looks so fragile. Her hair is a matted mess, her eyes are red and puffy from crying, and the circles under her eyes are darker than they were at lunch on Wednesday.

"I brought some cold and flu medicines and some nice hot chamomile tea."

She takes it from me without saying anything and goes back to watching what seems to be an infomercial.

I'm not sure exactly what to do. She won't look at me or talk to me, so I decide to join her on the couch and put my arm around her. She's stiff at first but soon relaxes into me, eventually succumbing to a silent cry. I don't press her on what's bothering her.

It takes some convincing, but I get her into the shower and open up her house. When she emerges, she looks better, but she's still not my Emerson. I can see she needs some sleep, but when I try to get her to her bedroom, she won't go. I offer to join her on the couch and while she rests, and reluctantly she agrees. I sit with her the rest of the morning and hold her. She puts her head down on my lap and quickly falls sound asleep. I can't find anything on television except a Harry Potter movie marathon, but I go with it so as not to disturb her.

It gets to be late afternoon and I'm hungry. I don't know what Emerson has in her fridge, so since she likes burgers, I order us a late lunch from an app on my cell phone and have it delivered. She wakes with a start when they ring the doorbell and Molly barks.

"Don't worry." I soothe her by rubbing her arm and speaking in a soft voice. "I ordered us some lunch. You need to eat, Emerson."

She seems disoriented from her nap and scared by the interruption. I wish she would tell me what has her scared. The smell of the burgers and fries fills her house, and Molly is begging with her big brown eyes. Emerson carefully looks at the burger, though it seems the smell wins her over when she takes a few small bites, eventually eating the whole thing.

"I can't believe I slept for so long. I haven't slept like that in weeks."

I can't help but think she even looks happier with a bit of sleep. And watching her eat her burger makes it almost as if the old Emerson is back.

After lunch, we go back to the Harry Potter marathon, though Emerson dozes as the movies play. Her phone pings, indicating a text message, and she groggily sits up and reads the text. I'm nosey and see it's from her friend CeCe.

You still up for dinner and drinks tonight?

I watch her type into her phone, Sorry. Work is overwhelming. Maybe next time. But before she can send it, I stop her.

"Em, I'd love to see CeCe again. Can I join you guys for drinks and dinner?"

She thinks about it a minute and texts, How about 6:30 at Hudson's? I'll have Dillon with me, if that's OK?

In seconds she replies, More than OK. See you then.

We watch more of our movie, and when it's time, I make sure she jumps in the shower again and gets ready for the night. When she comes out, she's stunning in a black sheath dress and the sandals I love. She looks fantastic, but the dress truly hangs on her. I'm becoming worried about her.

We stop by my place on our way to dinner so I can change. Hudson's is a good spot, but I can get away with a pressed pair of khakis paired with a red-and-white gingham dress shirt with the shirt sleeves rolled up and my brown Gucci loafers.

When we arrive, I see a group of women with CeCe, a look of relief covering her face. She hugs me and whispers in my ear, "Thank you for getting her out of the house."

Emerson's friends are giving her hugs and asking why she disappeared from their social scene. I hear them ask if we're dating and as she tells them we're only friends, I can't help but be a little disappointed, which is surprising to me as I don't usually want anyone to think I'm attached.

Turning my focus on CeCe, I speak in a low voice so no one can hear us. "I'm worried about Emerson. Do you know what's going on?"

Stepping back to look directly at me, she says, "She hasn't told you?"

"No, and I've asked directly. I keep begging for her to tell me, but she shuts down."

I don't get an answer from CeCe as Emerson walks up to join us. She looks absolutely radiant, her glow back.

CeCe tells her, "You look terrific Em."

She blushes. "Thanks. I got a bit of sleep today thanks to Dillon."

The other women exchange looks of "I told you so." Emerson is quick to set them straight, but they look like they're having a difficult time believing her.

Dinner is incredible, and we're loud and rowdy. CeCe is animated all night, quite outstanding at bringing Emerson into the conversation. We all work hard to get her laughing.

The restaurant is getting busy, so we agree it's time to head out. Emerson excuses herself to go to the bathroom, and CeCe leans over and hisses at me, "During the date with your asshole friend, he drugged her and date-raped her."

I am completely stunned by this news. I stutter, "Wh-what the. fuck? Adam?"

"Yesss. Emerson doesn't remember much, but she blames herself because she trusted him. Apparently, she excused herself to go to the bathroom, and we believe he must have put something in her drink because she doesn't remember anything else after that. She refused to report it because he was your friend."

My mind is racing. I've known Adam for over a decade. He was in my fraternity. We played football together. He's a good-looking guy and has no problems getting girls. I remember his college girlfriend, Melissa. She was a knockout. He always has a date. Why would he think he needed to date-rape my Emerson? I mutter more for myself than for CeCe, "Holy shit! How is she not upset with me? I introduced them."

Emerson walks up at that moment and asks, "Ready? I'm exhausted and want to head home."

I nod numbly, and we say our goodbyes to CeCe. Whispering in her ear during a quick hug, I assure her, "I'm going to kill that motherfucker. I promise."

"I'm counting on it."

THIRTEEN

DILLON

I'M FURIOUS. What the fuck was Adam thinking? I want to hear his version of the events and how he can explain his behavior, but I need to calm down a bit before I reach out to him or it'll get ugly, and most likely the police will get involved.

But first I need to take care of Emerson. She's been violated in the worst way. I make a few discreet calls and am able to find an excellent therapist for her and make an appointment. CeCe makes sure she goes, and after a few weeks, we finally see Emerson on the mend. Now I think it's time to get Adam's bullshit side of things.

> Dillon Healy: Dude! Haven't seen you in a while. Up for some basketball and drinks after work on Wednesday?
>
> Adam Stanton: Abso-fucking-lutely! 6 at the gym?
>
> Dillon Healy: See you then. Be prepared to get your ass kicked.
>
> Adam Stanton: Bring it on.

WE PLAY AND I'M INCREDIBLY AGGRESSIVE, Adam seeming a bit surprised by the rough play. I've knocked him down and thrown the ball hard at his testicles. He plays it off by asking, "Not getting laid? You've got a lot of anger, man."

I'm seeing him in a new light. He's talking about some girl he met last night and the great time they had. It seems like he's sleeping with a lot of girls, and I wonder if he's drugging them all.

After showers, we head to the Irish pub across the street from our gym and order a few beers.

I waited to talk to him, thinking it would help with my aggression, but I'm still incredibly angry. I can't be soft in my approach, so I'm direct. "So, tell me about your date with Emerson."

He's definitely uneasy, looking around at everything but me. "Why? Did she say anything?"

I want to shove my fist in his face. "Nope, but she's been avoiding me since."

"I hardly remember the date, so there must not have been much to tell."

It's taking all my willpower to stay calm, my hands tightly balled fists under the table. "So, you didn't get laid that night?"

With high confidence, he boasts, "Oh, I certainly got laid."

"She's a pretty conservative girl. I don't get the impression that she's one to sleep with someone on a first date, so how did you manage it?"

"Why so many questions? I have video if you don't believe me."

I blanch at the thought of Emerson being degraded on video. "Video? How did you get her to agree?" I know I can be a bit of a jerk when it comes to women, but I never force them to do anything they don't want, and I never record anything without their permission.

"She was into me, man. I think it turned her on that I was your friend."

"Why would *that* turn her on?"

"I dunno, man. Maybe she has the hots for you?"

"Did you slip her anything?"

"Man, I don't need to do that," he scoffs.

"Then why doesn't Emerson have any recollection of your night together?"

"She was fully into it and had a good time."

"You didn't answer my question. Did you drug Emerson?"

"No, man. I don't need any help getting women into bed."

"Then why doesn't she remember anything?

"No clue. I don't recall her drinking too much. Maybe she doesn't remember because she was blackout crazy for me. She begged me to get a room there at The Clift for some fun."

"She begged you? That doesn't sound like her at all. And she's beyond hot. Why would she need to beg you to do anything?"

"You sound a lot like a jealous boyfriend. She was a great lay. Go for it, man. You have my permission to take over."

Gritting my teeth, I hold my fists at my sides so tightly I think I've cut off the circulation to my fingers. "I don't need your permission. You fucking drugged Emerson. That's rape. You assaulted my partner and friend."

"It was entirely consensual. You can watch the video. Emerson is lying if she says I drugged her. What happened to 'bros over hos,' dude?"

I punch him right in the face. He rounds me off, and the next thing I know we've cleared the area and two big bouncers are separating us before kicking us out of the bar.

As I leave, people in a three-block radius hear me yell, "You motherfucker, you raped my best friend! You're going to pay for this!"

I grab a cab and take it directly to Emerson's house. I text her that I'm coming, but she doesn't respond. She doesn't answer my first knock either, but I know she's there. I can hear the television.

"Emerson, it's me. Dillon. Please open up. Please. I need to see you."

It takes a few minutes of my continued knocking until she finally opens the door.

She's dressed in sweatpants and a Yale Law hoodie. Her eyes are red-rimmed from crying, but they widen when she sees my right eye swollen shut and the blood all over my shirt. "Dillon! What happened? Are you okay?"

"I beat the shit out of Adam. I'm sorry. I didn't know. Please..." I don't know how to tell her that since I learned what happened, I entirely blame myself.

She opens the door wider and I embrace her, both crying. I want her to know she's safe, but I want her to tell me more, let me know how she feels so I can start to fix her hurt. I want to touch her, to soothe her, to take away the cloud that seems to surround her.

DILLON

*A*FTER THE INCIDENT with Adam, I call CeCe and we agree to meet for coffee at a local French café not too far from our offices. I arrive first and secure us a table in the back. The décor is a bit cheesy with lots of Eiffel Towers and French flags, but the pain au chocolate and croissants, plus the coffee and espresso drinks are the best in The City.

CeCe walks into the coffee shop with not a hair out of place. Her perfect light pink manicure looks great against her dark gray boiled wool long jacket over a matching dark gray T-shirt, black pants, and a sexy pair of black sandals. She greets me with a hug and orders herself a drink before reaching toward my eye, which is still a bit green.

"I was so angry. I punched Adam in the face, but he got a good swing in before the bouncers separated us." She laughs but I lean in and tell her, "I'm most concerned that he has it on video."

Her hand goes to her mouth. "Are you kidding me? Video? What are we going to do?"

Her drink arrives and I sit patiently, waiting to tell her my plan until the waiter is out of earshot. Leaning in so no one around us can hear, I whisper, "I have an idea. It borders on illegal, so I need a sane person to talk me out of it."

"Then you've come to the wrong person, my friend," she says as she reaches for my arm.

"Well, listen first. Emerson can't have been the first person he's done this to."

Contemplating what I've said, she takes a small sip of her cappuccino. "Agreed."

"Don't you know someone in the district attorney's office?"

She stirs her drink. "You mean the district attorney?"

Sitting back, I cross my legs. "Yeah, him."

"I've known him most of my life. What are you thinking?"

"Well, I do have a few hacker friends who are black hats."

"Black hats?"

"They do illegal hacking," I explain.

Looking around to make sure no one in the coffee shop is listening, she urges, "Okay, keep going."

"Well, he said the video is on his phone, which means it's most likely backed up on the cloud, so if we steal his phone, it doesn't destroy the video."

Glancing up at the ceiling and with a deep breath, she says, "Sometimes I hate technology."

"We could get someone to go in and delete his cloud, then steal his computer, tablet, and cell phone so it's entirely gone and erased."

"I'm liking this."

"I'm thinking we could take the video to your friend, and if we find any others in the process, maybe they could arrest him for being a serial rapist."

She takes a few moments, then finally says, "I like it, but they would need to know how we came into possession of the evidence. Then the girls would all have to testify."

Sitting back, I try to not show all the disappointment I feel. "That's what I'm afraid of. Then we'll have to go with plan B. We have our black hats ruin him."

"I'm still interested. What are you thinking?"

"His credit cards all get maxed, his credit is destroyed, his condo goes into foreclosure, he's listed on all those pedophile websites... and whatever else we can think of."

Laughing, CeCe says, "Remind me never to cross you. I think I'm comfortable with getting the videos off the cloud and maybe have his phone, tablet, and computer find water. Less comfortable with destroying him."

"I like the way you think."

"That's why you're a good partner in crime." Taking a drink of my coffee, I look out the window. "She's kind and gentle. It kills me that Adam destroyed her spirit."

"I agree, but I'm hoping it only went away and will come back once we get some of this behind her."

EMERSON

6 months later

$\mathcal{I}$T'S JUST AFTER 4:30 P.M. and I'm working my way home on the bus. My mind is busy with my mental to-do list of what I need to get accomplished. I know I should write it all down, but I can't bring myself to dig out a pad and paper. The worst part is I know as I'm in the shower, I'll remember what I forgot to do because I didn't write it down.

The bus is crowded with people making their way from downtown out into the San Francisco city neighborhoods. There's something magical about being one of many sitting on the bus, an easing to the loneliness within. We act the same, move at the same moment, and we watch the city move around us. Everyone is in their own world, earbuds in their ears and ignoring everything and everyone around them with blank and exhausted looks on each of our faces. As I look out the windows, I see it's a gray day—it isn't foggy but dreary. I'm looking forward to heading into Palo Alto for some sunshine this weekend and a round of golf.

As I dream of sunny blue skies and warm days, my cell phone rings—CeCe. "Hey, chica! What's up?"

"Hey! I'm in your hood and wanted to see if you could escape for a cup of coffee. I'd have you back to your dungeon in an hour."

I can hear her need to talk, and I'm tempted. "By my office?"

"Yep."

I feel a twinge of guilt for ignoring my friend these past few weeks. I seem to be spending every waking minute outside of the office with Dillon. I need to make it up to her somehow. "So enticing, but I've left for the day. But...."

"What? You don't leave until it's been dark for a few hours."

"I do, too. All the time. Dillon and I go running several evenings a week. Right now I'm on Muni, and it's crowded. This is why I don't leave when the rest of the world leaves."

"Where are you off to? Hot date with Dillon?"

I laugh at even the notion of a date. "No! I'm headed to my therapist appointment. Dillon's going to pick me up afterward and we'll go for a run, but you do know we're only friends."

"You both can't breathe without each other. Just do the deed and get married already."

"You're funny. Dillon doesn't like me *that* way. I'm another sister to him, and he's a brother to me." I don't need or desire the lecture about my relationship with Dillon. I'm attracted to him, but he's kept me at arm's length. I'm grateful for everything he's done for me, so I'm not willing to risk anything by pushing for more than what we have now.

"Honey, do you sleep in the same bed night after night with your brothers?"

"CeCe, we don't sleep together 'night after night.' Please remember, we've both signed explicit non-fraternization clauses. We can only be friends. Good friends, but only friends."

Changing subjects, she asks, "How are things going with your therapist?"

"You know, when you set up the first appointment, it was tough to tell her about what happened and how I blamed myself. But she's been amazing. I can sleep at night again, and I feel as if good things are coming out of our conversations. Honestly, I think she wants to release me, but we get along so well it's like meeting with a friend."

"What does she say about your relationship with Dillon?"

My therapist thinks Dillon is important to me and encourages me to explore more, but I won't admit that to CeCe. "We haven't talked much about him for a while."

"Okay, so you're holding back on her."

"I'm at my stop. I've got to go. Can I call you later?"

"Of course! And I promise I won't harp on you about this anymore. I love you."

"I love you, too."

"See you Saturday after golf with Dillon?"

"I think we're getting all of us to play together. Want to join us?"

"All the partners, including Sara?"

"Yep. We could make it the three girls against the three guys?"

"Count me in."

DILLON ARRIVES AT CECE'S PLACE at six thirty Saturday morning. We stopped and picked up coffee on the way, as I promised when we made our tee time. I hand her a cup as she gets in the car wearing light pink walking shorts, a white polo shirt and a green, pink, and white argyle sweater vest. Her chestnut hair is pulled back in a ponytail, topped by a white Stanford visor. She looks so put together.

"Thank you for stopping for coffee." Breathing in the scent and taking her first sip, CeCe says, "This tastes amazing. I can't believe you guys do this almost every Saturday." Bitterly, she adds, "No one is awake at six thirty in the morning on a Saturday."

Dillon loads her clubs with mine and joins us in the car. "CeCe, regular human beings are asleep when you go to bed at two o'clock in the morning."

"Harrumph. Plenty of people are still awake at two. But I'm trying to be more of a morning person these days," she tells us.

We drive in silence as Dillon maneuvers his SUV out of The City and onto Highway 101. I turn around and see she's staring out the window. "Should we put together a plan on how we're going to beat the guys today?"

"I plan to let you play every shot while I drink a lot of mimosas and look cute," she tells me with a big grin.

"You always look cute." I turn to Dillon. "Are we playing best ball or adding all of our scores up? You guys were going to figure it out."

"I think we'll be adding all the scores."

I look at CeCe in the rearview mirror. "You may have to swing a club today."

She nods. "I can do that, too."

"You seem nervous. Is everything all right?"

She looks at me and smiles big. "Of course. I'm just not used to being up so early. This is going to be a lot of fun."

Arriving at the club, I see Sarah and Mason exiting Cameron's SUV. We girls make our way to the driving range before our 7:35 a.m. tee time. Dillon worked it out with the starter to allow us to play as a group of six. So at least we'll be all together.

Apparently, Dillon and I will be riding together and playing off the back tees. Mason and CeCe will be riding together and playing from the middle tees, and Cameron and Sara will be riding together and playing off the front tees. The goal is to each play our best, and the winners are the lowest combined score. We're playing girls versus boys, as well as a secondary competition between those driving together. Cameron has indicated there may be prizes for Worst Shot, Hole-in-Ones and Best Trick Shot.

We're going to have a great time.

DILLON

*T*HE GUYS are counting on me to pull this out for them. My handicap requires me to play off the back tees, so it'll increase the challenge. CeCe is probably better at the front tees, so it should help even us up.

When we start off, we let Emerson go first, and her shot is beautiful. I can only hope my shot is equally as good. As I hit my ball, I know it's not going to get the distance Emerson got, but I'm grateful it's in the middle and not off in the trees.

CeCe and Mason pull up to the middle tees, and after she takes some direction from him, she swings and hits the ball. It outruns mine. Looking at Mason, she asks, "Did it meet your requirements?"

Turning to the group, Mason says, "I think the girls have pulled the wool over our eyes." He shoots his ball and it goes a bit farther than all of ours, but he's in a wooded area, which may be more challenging to get out of.

Sara is next from the front tees. Her shot isn't as far as the previous ones, maybe twenty yards behind Emerson and fifteen yards behind CeCe, but she's right down the middle. Cameron stands and takes the worst swing I've ever seen, his ball finding the water next to the tee box. He looks at us all sheepishly. "Did I mention that Sara and I get two do-overs every nine holes?"

I laugh the loudest. "You mean mulligans?"

Cameron and Sara look at the rest of us and nod.

We end the first nine holes pretty close. Emerson's short game helps to keep the girls in the running, and CeCe only struggles on longer holes, but she's a top-notch player. Sara and Cameron are having fun, which is all that matters.

The back nine holes, I completely crumble. I'm over par on all nine—meaning I'm over at least one shot per hole. The women win the game by almost ten strokes. As we drink our Bloody Marys and mimosas and the women celebrate their win, Cameron taps his glass with a spoon.

CeCe, looking at me, asks, "Do we kiss our partners now?"

Cameron tells her, "You and Mason are more than welcome to kiss. We won't stop you."

CeCe blushes a deep shade of pink and we all laugh at her embarrassment. Mason smiles.

Cameron allows the ribbing to die down and then places a box and three items on the table behind him. He's commanding the attention of the entire bar, and he announces as if he's reading for an awards show on television, "The award nominees for Worst Shot are—drum roll please—Dillon's epic meltdown on the last nine holes. Didn't you tell us your game was improving and you thought you could probably beat Emerson?"

The group is laughing as I sputter, "No! I didn't say that!" I turn to Emerson, trying not to laugh at being caught. "Really, I never said anything like that."

Cameron shakes his head, and mutters, "We know where your loyalties are—just wait." After the room settles down, Cameron continues. "Mason's superpowered putting and missing multiple easy shots on the third, seventh, sixteenth, seventeenth, and eighteenth holes."

We're all laughing while Mason denies he had so many poor shots. "Hey! I'll give you the last three holes, but it was the pressure CeCe was putting on me. She was supposed to be a lousy player like me, but she's actually surprisingly good."

CeCe turns to him, pushes on his shoulder, and says, "That's what you get. You failed to notice I played golf at Stanford, too."

Everyone seems stunned by this comment until CeCe mutters, "I didn't say I was on the golf team, I just said I played." And she winks at Emerson.

"Get a room," Dillon tells Mason and CeCe, which only encourages the rest of us to laugh.

Cameron tries to take control back and says, "And the third nominee for Worst Shot is me, as I went through nineteen balls today."

"Nineteen? You counted?" Sara asks, seeming confused.

"Of course I counted. I guess I bought the box of balls that are magnetized to water."

We all debate the winner, and with a lot of arguing and the offer of pay-offs, we agree as a group that Cameron wins first place and the trophy. He proudly places the homemade trophy of a glass of water with a ball that has grass stuck to it on the bottom. On the placard, he writes his name, the date, and "19 Balls & Counting."

Other people in the bar are laughing and sharing their opinion. A few can be heard asking if they can join us the next time we have a tournament.

Sara pipes up, "Okay, what award is next?"

Cameron takes his cue. "So, we had a few good trick shots. The nominees are Emerson's shot on the sixth hole, where she hit a ball on the fringe of the water backward and it landed a foot from the cup. The second is Sara's one-handed forty-foot putt from across the green. And the final nomination goes to Dillon's vicious shot from the pine on the thirteenth hole, which shot the ball deep in the sand in the bunker."

"Hey, at least the tree kept the ball from going out of bounds," I reply.

Maybe it's the alcohol, or perhaps we're all being silly, but we vote the award goes to me.

Cameron hands me a homemade trophy with a golf ball that has been ripped open from too much stress, hand-painted gold, and placed prominently on a piece of wood. Taking a black Sharpie marker, he customizes a front placard with my name, the date, and the hole before handing it to me.

Mason prods Cameron to continue. "We have a special award for Sara."

Everyone turns to look at Sara, who's turning bright pink from her embarrassment.

"Sara, we never knew you played. You're welcome to join us anytime. Here is an award for being gracious when we were jerks."

Emerson chants, "Hear! Hear!"

Cameron hands Sara a real trophy of a gold woman in a long dress with a sash and crown. Probably for a beauty queen winner, but it works perfectly for Sara.

She looks at it and exclaims, "It's a real trophy with my name even engraved on the front. Thank you, guys. Really. This means a lot to me." She walks around and gives each of the partners a warm embrace. When she gets to CeCe, she says, "I can't leave you out," and they hug.

CeCe asks, "Did anyone hit a hole-in-one?"

Cameron shakes his head. "Thank goodness, too, because usually you win a car for a hole-in-one. I only have my car, and frankly, I'd have no way to get Sara, Mason, and me back into The City."

CeCe speaks up, "Don't worry, Cameron. We would have called you a Lyft."

As everyone laughs, Cameron taps a spoon to the side of a glass to regain our attention. "We have another round of prizes in the pair competition." He takes three bottles of liquor out of the box. "We all knew Emerson would kill all of us, so for her we have a 2007 Dom Perignon White Gold Champagne for beating Dillon."

There is a lot of "Hear! Hear!" and laughing. I can only shake my head.

Cameron continues, "And in Cart 2, the winner between CeCe and Mason is CeCe! For your win, we have a bottle of Grape Boones Farm Wine—vintage last week. Enjoy!"

CeCe is laughing harder than anyone. "Believe it or not, I like this. It tastes like grape cold medicine but it's not that bad!"

Cameron, trying to take control of the group once more, taps his glass with his spoon, and says, "For Cart 1, the lowest score by over 23 strokes is Sara!" He is holding a bottle of peach schnapps.

Sara laughs as she stands to take her prize. "I'd like to thank the Academy and Cameron for making my win so easy."

Cameron gives her a big hug and says, "I have orange juice should anyone wish to share!"

We spend another hour enjoying ourselves before heading back. It was a perfect event for us and well needed.

DILLON

*M*Y LANDLINE IS RINGING at home, my parents' number on the caller ID. *It's after midnight. Why is anyone calling me at this hour?*

Answering half-asleep and not thinking it's anything more than a late-night check-in, I mumble, "Hello?"

"Dillon, your dad had a heart attack tonight and is at the hospital. It isn't good." My mom is crying into the phone as she speaks. "Can you come home?"

I'm fully awake and immediately alert. "Of course. I'll get a flight as soon as I can." Mom continues weeping into the phone, and I ask, "Have you talked to Siobhan?"

"She's loading the car and will drive up. She'll be here tomorrow with Steven."

"Mom, Dad is healthy. He's going to be okay. I'll get with the airlines and get to you as soon as I can. As soon as I have the details, I'll call you." I sit up in bed and begin looking for a pair of pants.

"Dillon, I'm scared."

"I know, Mom. Me, too. We need to have faith. He's strong and is going to be fine." I listen to her cry as I bring up my computer and go to the Delta website. "Mom there is a 7:00 a.m. flight out of SFO direct into Detroit. I land at three thirty, and I'll have a car service bring me up to the hospital in Birmingham. I'll be with you before dinner tonight. Hang on, and be sure to tell Dad and Siobhan I'll be there soon." I go through the motions to book the flight, knowing I have only a short time before I have to be at the airport if I'm going to make this flight.

"Dillon, thank you." She continues to cry but hangs up.

I'm out of bed and now scrambling. Grabbing a bag, I quickly pack it with more than what I'll need, though I make the decision to not bring a suit. I want to think positive. I stuff a massive stack of underwear, socks, and shirts in my bag, plus two pairs of jeans. Hopping in and out the shower, I put on a pair of jeans, a T-shirt, and a fleece cover. Grabbing my Gucci loafers and my Dopp kit, I zip up my bag as the car service rings they've arrived. I think I have everything; what I forgot I can buy while there.

On the drive to the airport, I leave a message for each of the partners on their office phones repeating what's going on and asking different tasks from each.

As I sit in the airport lounge awaiting my flight, I call Emerson. She answers groggily and I know I woke her.

"Hey. My mom called last night. My dad had a heart attack," I choke out.

"Oh no! Is he okay?" she asks, sounding a little more awake.

I'm barely holding back tears. "He's in the hospital. I'm at the airport. My flight takes off in less than two hours. I land before three thirty. I have a car service picking me up and taking me directly to the hospital."

"What can I do for you while you're gone?" She's alert and thinking despite the early hour.

"I left messages for everyone with directions. You know what's going on with my portfolio of clients." I start to lose it, and I don't want the people sitting around me to see me cry. Looking out the window, watching the horizon begin to lighten and all the activity on the tarmac, I run my hand through my hair and choke out, "I can't believe this. My dad is active and healthy. How can this be happening to him?"

Her throat catches as she says, "Oh, Dillon. My heart is breaking for you. I'm sure he's going to be fine. Do you want me to meet you there?"

I would love to have her join me, but I can't do that right now. "No. I need my dad to get better."

"Stay strong for your mom and keep me posted," she insists.

How is it that just talking to her makes me feel better? I want to have a conversation with Mason and Cameron about the fraternization clause. It would be nice if it would go away. But at the same time, I'm not good at relationships. What would I do if I screwed up with Emerson, causing it all to go sideways?

THE FLIGHT SEEMS LONGER THAN USUAL. I'm flying first-class and nervous about not getting to my dad fast enough. I must have looked at my watch every three minutes. Of course, I'm on the only plane where the Wi-Fi is down, which only increases my anxiety. I'm out of touch for a four-hour flight. I forgot my tablet, and I didn't download any entertainment, so I'm left to wait impatiently. The flight attendant offers me drinks, but I want to be fully cognizant when I arrive.

As we land, my cell phone finally has service and goes crazy with emails and voice mails. I work my way through to the arrivals area and see a livery driver holding a placard with my name. I'm surprised for a half second that it's a woman, and she tells me her name is Heidi. She takes my bag and we head out to the curb. When I made the reservation this morning, I had to give them the address, so she already knows where we're going. Luckily we're ahead of the crazy Detroit afternoon traffic as we head northeast to Royal Oak and the hospital. During the forty-five-minute drive, I listen to my voice mails.

Mason, Sara, and Cameron have updates and assurances that what I need from them will be taken care of, and they wish my dad a speedy recovery.

I'm surprised to have a message from CeCe. "Dillon, Emerson told me your news. I'm thinking about you and want you to know that you and your family are in my thoughts."

Emerson's voice mail means the most to me. "Hey. Everything here is going well. Molly and I both already miss you. I know your dad is proud of you. We have work covered, so don't give us a second thought. Let me know if there's anything I can do, and I'll check in with you later. Be strong."

I arrive at the hospital and walk immediately up to my dad's room. My mom looks frail and tiny as she sits in the sterile hospital room, holding my sleeping dad's hand. In jeans with a white shirt under a blue button-up sweater, she looks very put together despite the ordeal. Her blue eyes are red-rimmed and puffy from crying.

I bring her in for a big hug, and she weeps. "He's the love of my life. I can't live without him. You've got to make him understand that I'm not ready to face this world without him. Make him understand."

I hold her and look at my dad. He's sleeping with a thousand tubes and wires attached to his arms and chest. "Don't worry, Mom," I assure her. "I'll talk to him. I need him, too, and I'm not ready either."

I encourage my mom to go for a walk, get some air or coffee, and I sit down next to dad, holding his hand. "Please, Dad. Not yet," I choke out just above a whisper. "Please don't leave me yet. I need you so much."

I don't know if I imagine it, but I feel him grip my hand, and then the tears fall relentlessly like a dam has been released. A few of my parents' friends stop by and kindly take my mom to eat some dinner. She insists she'll be in the downstairs cafeteria with her cell phone "at the ready" if she's needed, and I nod in acknowledgment.

Shortly after eight, my sister, Siobhan, arrives with her husband, Steven, trailing behind her. Her eyes are swollen from crying. She sits in the chair on the other side of our father and puts her head down on his shoulder. She also begs him not to die.

My dad wakes for a few minutes, though he's weak and sounds frail. Turning to my sister, he rasps, "I couldn't have asked for a better daughter. You've always been the light of my world. I love you. Continue making a difference with those kids you teach. They are the future. Please tell the kids how much I love them, and that I'll be in heaven looking out for them."

She hugs him and is crying nonstop. Arguing with him to not

give up, she tells him she's newly pregnant and he needs to be there to meet his new grandchild.

He squeezes both of our hands, then looks at me and tells me, "Dillon, I'm proud of everything you've accomplished. You'll be a success at whatever you put your mind to. I want you to remember that money isn't everything. Find a nice girl and start a family. You'll be an amazing father. Take care of your mother and sister. Your mom and Siobhan are going to need you to be strong. I love you, too."

Not ready to let him go, I decide to tell him all about Emerson. "Dad, she's smart and funny. You'd like her. And she's an amazing golfer. You need to play with her. We could fool so many of your golf buddies."

He smiles and lightly squeezes my hand once more.

My mom has been standing in the back of the room, and there isn't a dry eye anywhere. Even a tear escapes my dad's right eye. His breathing becomes shallow and the grip on my hand loses its strength. We hear the heart monitor go to a flatline, and nurses come running in an attempt to revive him without success.

We all stand here stunned, our hearts broken.

"How can this be?" my mother cries as she sobs into her hands. The three of us cry together. We aren't ready to say goodbye.

Please, Dad, come back. I need you. Who am I going to talk to? Who's going to support me? Who's going to take care of all of us?

OUR FAMILY PRIEST arrived during the confusion. He gives my dad last rites, and we're all numb. He counsels us a bit about my father's death, but I'm on autopilot.

Looking at my watch, I'm stunned to see it's shortly after midnight. I don't know what to do with myself. Siobhan has Steven, and though my mom is a walking zombie, she's with family friends who are comforting her between talking to the hospital administrators about next steps. I need comfort, and the only thing I can think of is speaking with Emerson.

Nothing makes sense anymore, not even trees. My dad's life had direction and meaning. All his work has been for my mom and their life together. Now he's gone, there's no reason for the world to exist anymore, so why is it all still here?

I'm sitting alone with my dad and I can't move. My dad was talking to me. I was telling him about Emerson. My Emerson.

Without warning, I feel my insides become wooden and cold. I'm tapped on the shoulder and look up at a gentleman in hospital scrubs. "Mr. Healy, we need to take the body down to the morgue. You're welcome to stay, or you can go now."

I only want to talk to one person. I walk into an empty room and call Emerson. With the time difference, it isn't as late for her.

In a soft and calming voice, she says, "Hi. How are you doing?"

"Not good. I got to see my dad, and we talked for a few minutes, but he...." My voice cracks and I choke up.

"Oh, Dillon. I'm so sorry. Are you okay?"

"No. I'm not prepared for this. My dad is my best friend. He's been my biggest cheerleader my whole life. I don't know what to do."

"I'm so sorry," she says, and then we cry together over the phone.

EMERSON

$\mathcal{M}$ Y HEART IS BREAKING for Dillon. I haven't lost a parent, and I can't even imagine how he's feeling. Despite the late hour, I call Sara, Mason, and Cameron and give them the news. We're all stunned, agreeing we want to attend any services to support Dillon and his family. Cameron and Mason have met Dillon's dad on several occasions, and they're heartbroken.

I have a difficult night of sleep, knowing Dillon is hurting but now how I can help to make it better. I hit a bucket of golf balls in the morning, arriving just as the golden glow of the sun hits the horizon. It does help to relieve the tension in my shoulders, but not much else.

I figure I need to find out when the services will be held and see what we can do as a firm. When I get to work, we all grieve as a group. Mason sends an email out to the company with the announcement while I make a few calls and carefully find out what details I can get about the wake and funeral.

In all the craziness, Dillon tells me where I can find a key to his apartment, then asks me to grab one of his suits. He is very specific in his directions: the black summer wool Armani suit, the white shirt with French cuffs bearing his initials in light blue, his silver cuff links that his dad wore on his wedding day, his light blue tie, a pair of black socks, and his Ferragamo black loafers.

Walking into his apartment seems like trespassing. I've been here many times but always with him. It's a penthouse apartment in a building built in the early nineteen hundreds overlooking Alcatraz, the Golden Gate Bridge and the northern portion of the bay. It's been completely refurbished with sixteen-foot ceilings, ornate crown molding, and beautiful hardwood floors. The kitchen is modern with dark granite counter tops and sleek white cabinets, the furniture black leather and contemporary. While Dillon's tall, he always seems to take up the entire room, so his apartment feels big when he isn't here.

His closet is larger than my bedroom and is lined with more clothes than even I have. I'm a bit surprised when I see he has probably a dozen suits, considering I've never seen him in one. It takes a few minutes of my combing through his things to find what he needs, especially since I take the time to photograph each garment and text him the pictures to make sure I have exactly what he's looking for. His reply to each text is a brief Yes, nothing more.

Finding his mailbox key next to his door, I decide to grab his mail and bring it with me, unsure how long he plans on staying in Michigan. I quickly water his three plants before I walk out.

I text him one more time. The partners and I are flying in on a NetJet tomorrow. Can I bring you anything else?

I look for a few things to keep me busy when my phone rings.

"You guys don't need to come," Dillon states. "Business is much more important. You're all needed there, not here with my dad's crazy friends and my family."

I can hear the hurt in his voice and softly tell him, "You're important to all of us. Please don't feel the need to entertain us or spend time with us. We're coming to support you and your family. We have a reservation in Birmingham at a cute spot. We'll entertain ourselves. We'll arrive tomorrow afternoon." I'm almost positive he's crying. "Please let me know what I can do, or if you would like anything else from your apartment. I miss you."

THE ENTIRE COMPANY IS SOMBER. Annabel, at reception, sends an email out that she's going to collect money for a donation in Dillon's dad's name to be given to the American Heart Association. She stresses it isn't mandatory, and even loose change is appreciated.

Mason follows up with an email stating he will match whatever anyone donates. Cameron piles on and impresses giving isn't required, but because his good friend Mason wants to match, he's giving five thousand dollars. The exchange helps everyone's spirits rise on such a somber occasion. In the end, we have a check for almost twenty thousand dollars. Cameron is clearly moved by the gesture of so many, writing a gracious thank-you email to Annabel for thinking about Dillon and his family, and to everyone who donated.

Mason has a client in his portfolio who has a share of a NetJet. He called him and explained what happened with Dillon, asking if he could pay to "rent" his share of the Learjet for the flight out to Detroit; we would then take commercial flights back at the end of the week. The client graciously gave us his share and insisted we take it roundtrip at no cost to us.

Flying in a private jet is the ultimate luxury. If it were under better circumstances, I would've taken in the opulence of the experience. Instead, I sit in my chair and cry almost the entire flight. Sara eats the Dean & DeLuca Swedish Fish, and Cameron and Mason work on the scotch in the minibar and all the pretzels they can find. It's somber, and we all feel for Dillon.

Our rental car is sitting at the base of the jet bridge, and we load up and head into Birmingham.

I text Dillon to let him know we've arrived. Hey, we're here and staying at the Townsend. We'd love to see you. We're going to find someplace to eat if you and anyone else would like to join us.

He replies, My favorite pizza place is Anthony's and is within walking distance from your hotel. Can I meet you there in about two hours?

See you then.

Sharing the news with everyone, we agree on pizza for dinner. When Dillon walks in, he looks haggard. He sits next to me and holds my hand under the table. We enjoy a fantastic Chicago-style pizza, a wonderful thick crust with a layer of spicy tomato sauce. The pie we ordered has layers of meats, onions, olives, and a gooey layer of cheese, which we enjoy with a few too many beers. We avoid the elephant in the room and instead discuss the Detroit Tigers and their struggling season for over three hours.

When we move from the pizza joint to the hotel bar, Sara heads up to her room, and I join the guys drinking a club soda. They seem determined to drink themselves sloppy. I request of

Dillon, "Please, grab a room here tonight or a cab back to your mom's."

He salutes me, and I head upstairs. After a while, I realize I can't sleep, and my book isn't grabbing my attention, so I dress in my workout clothes and head to the hotel gym, setting the elliptical for a forty-five-minute session.

I'm almost done when my phone rings—Dillon. "They don't have any rooms. Can I stay with you?"

Without even thinking about it, I tell him, "Of course. I'm in room 412, but I'm in the gym finishing my workout. You can come grab the key, or I can get you in the bar in about ten minutes."

"No problem. I'll be waiting for you at the bar."

I finish my workout and dry off a bit before I go in search of Dillon. He's sitting in the corner of the bar all by himself. "Hey. You ready?"

He nods and follows me. I can tell he's drunk, so I hold his hand and direct him toward my room as he slightly stumbles and sways a bit. I help him remove his pants, leaving his boxer shorts and a T-shirt on. Tucking him into bed, I'm able to talk him into two Advil and a big glass of water.

"I would've liked my dad to meet you. I told him about you before he died. He...." Dillon has passed out mid-sentence.

I tuck him in, take a shower, and then work a few hours before turning in myself. We've shared a bed multiple times but never did anything beyond cuddle. I get under the covers and shimmy up to him.

He holds me tightly and whispers, "I don't know what I would do without you."

His comment makes me happy and content. I think the same of him. He's my rock in every storm.

EMERSON

THE WAKE is at the funeral home. It can be disconcerting if you aren't Catholic and aren't prepared to see the deceased laid out alongside people talking, drinking, and celebrating their life. Dillon comes from an Irish Catholic family, and it's definitely an Irish wake—lots of Irish whiskey is flowing, and people are definitely having a good time. "To Liam!" can be heard over and over as people toast to him and drink their whiskey.

When the four of us wander into the room, people stop their conversations and stare. Cameron sings the Sesame Street song loud enough for the four of us to hear, "One of these things is not like the others" and Sara and I giggle. Mason leads us as we walk past Dillon's dad, and I make the sign of the cross and place my hand on my heart while saying a small prayer.

I never met Dillon's dad, but I'm crying as if I'd known him forever. I guess it's because I know how hard this is for Dillon and his family. Standing at the end of the casket, Dillon, his mom, Siobhan, and her husband, Steven, are receiving guests.

Mason speaks to each person, sharing sweet stories about Dillon and his dad. Sara is next and gives each of them a sincere hug, telling them how sorry she is for their loss.

My eyes are red-rimmed as I hug Dillon. I tell him, "Your dad was proud of you. I'm sorry." He hugs me back, clearly too choked up to say anything. He's a broken man. As I embrace Dillon's mom and sister, I say, "I'm sorry for your loss. I'm also sorry I never had the chance to meet him. Dillon speaks fondly of his family. I know it's a real loss."

After Cameron goes through and, like Mason, shares funny stories about Dillon's dad with each of them, none of us has dry eyes. His mother pulls us in for another hug and shares, "This means so much to Dillon, Siobhan, and me that you came from so far away. Thank you."

There is Irish whiskey for everyone. Dillon's uncle gives a toast to his brother in Gaelic which most of us don't understand. We enjoy visiting and everyone telling beautiful stories. Dillon is by my side most of the time.

Everyone is somewhat drunk before dinner. Sara and I are drinking club soda and visiting with one another. "How are things with Henry?"

She gets teary. "We broke up a few weeks ago."

I gently pat her arm. "Oh no. I'm so sorry. Henry sounded promising."

She tries to smile as if it's a fact of life. "It was, but he failed to mention that he was married. Once I found out, I broke it off with him."

With a hand on each of her shoulders, I look directly at her. "Sara, you're beautiful, smart, and an amazing catch. You de-

VENTURE CAPITALIST • FORBIDDEN LOVE

serve a guy who is single and one hundred percent available to you. I know there is a great guy out there for you."

Wiping tears from her eyes, she tells me, "I see why Dillon is in love with you."

Surprised by such an out-of-context statement, I sputter, "He's not in love with me. We're just friends."

She smiles at me with a twinkle in her eyes as she reaches for my hand. "He may not have admitted it to himself or to you, but he is in love with you. And you two belong together."

Cameron walks up so I can't continue the conversation, though I keep replaying it as I meet uncles, aunts, friends, and neighbors.

As I look around, I spot Dillon standing alone at the over-flowing buffet table and walk over.

Trying to be funny, I ask, "Anything to eat around here?"

Turning, he smiles at me. "Just a little bit."

I put my hand on his arm and squeeze. "What a beautiful tribute to your dad."

"Thank you. He would've been embarrassed, but I liked it."

I watch him pick at the food, not sure what to put on his plate. "You know, you have many of the traits they shared about your dad."

Dillon blushes a beautiful shade of crimson. "I don't know about that. My dad was pretty special."

I point to a picture that was taken of his father at a similar age to Dillon now and whisper, "You look like him, too. He bragged about you to all his friends. He was proud of you and Siobhan."

Turning to me, he looks around and asks, "Can I stay with

you again tonight? I can't sleep at my parents' house."

"Of course. You can come home with us in our car, or you can take a cab over later. But promise me you won't drive."

He holds up three fingers like a Boy Scout. "I promise."

As WE LEAVE, I hug Dillon goodbye and whisper in his ear, "I slipped my room key in your pocket."

"I won't be long."

WE DRIVE BACK to the hotel and, not ready to go back to our rooms, we walk into the bar. The crowd this evening is young and hip, a combination of men and women in all shapes and sizes, dressed in dark suits as if they're coming from a funeral, too. But the conversation is formal, a get-to-know-you-professionally kind of talking. Clearly a networking event. They seem to all be drinking wines and bottled beer.

Sara leans in. "Do you think if we told them who some of our investment clients were, we could be popular with this crowd?"

We all laugh because we know she's right.

We find a table in the back corner, the waitress takes our order, and we make idle chitchat. Once our drinks arrive, the conversation naturally moves as if we've been friends forever.

Mason shares, "I've broken up with my girlfriend."

"I'm sorry," Sara and I say in unison.

"You know, I'm not. Look at the relationship Dillon's parents have. That's what I want."

We all nod, understanding exactly what he means.

Cameron tells some funny stories an uncle shared about Dillon as a teenager. "Apparently his mom came home from something and he was in the shower with a girl. She walked in and demanded the girl leave, then waited for Dillon to get out of the shower."

"You're kidding," Sara laughs.

"No, I'm not," Cameron insists. "His uncle said that Dillon's mom then gave him a lecture for over an hour about safe sex."

We hadn't realized Dillon had walked up until he adds, "It was actually a lecture about her not wanting to be a grandmother before forty."

We all laugh at that.

"Celeste was there today. I'm sure she wasn't happy that story was being told." He continues, "Following the incident, my mom went out and bought me a box of condoms. Let me assure you, using condoms your mom bought is ideal for safe sex." Sensing our confusion, he explains, "I couldn't use condoms my mom bought me. It meant I couldn't have sex again until they all expired. It was too weird for me. And boy, was Celeste pissed!"

We all laughed so hard we were crying.

I ask the guys, "What would your parents do if they'd walked in on you taking a shower with your girlfriend?"

Cameron laughs and says, "I don't think she would've bought me a box of condoms, that's for sure." Pausing for a few seconds, he continues, "I think she'd have yelled loud enough that three towns away could hear her."

We look at Mason expectantly, and he shares, "My mom wouldn't have liked it, but honestly, I didn't have my first girlfriend until I was a freshman at Stanford."

"I find that hard to believe," Sara chimes in.

Mason turns and says, "Okay, what about you two?"

"I have four older brothers, so there is no way he would've gotten into the house, let alone the bathroom alone with me." I tell him.

Chuckling, we all turn to Sara.

"I was living with a foster family at that point and they probably wouldn't have cared," she shares. "But don't let that be a downer. My parents passed away when I was five, and I was moved from foster family to foster family. The one I had in high school still looks out for me today. They're a wonderful older couple who could never have kids, and they were very open-minded."

Cameron, clearly sensing Sara is uncomfortable, turns to Dillon and asks, "Hey, man, you staying here at the Townsend?"

"Yeah, I got a room last night. I can't sleep at my mom's. I can hear her crying in her room, and it kills me."

"We were talking about what a great relationship your parents had," I tell him. "It's something we all want."

Dillon puts his arm around me and gives me a hug. "Thanks. What they had was special." We all sit there a moment, not sure what to say. "I guess I'm bringing the party down. What's everyone going to do tomorrow morning? Sleep in?"

Sara gets a text and excuses herself.

Mason shares, "Cameron and I are talking about heading over to the Ford Museum."

Dillon nods his approval. "Great place for the car junkies in both of you."

"Sara and I are thinking about wandering the zoo," I tell him.

"I haven't been to the zoo since I was a kid. It should be fun."

"You're welcome to join us. "

The guys order a round of drinks and I excuse myself. I need to go work out some of the stress I'm feeling. "Are we meeting for breakfast?"

"Sure, eight?" Mason asks.

"See you then. Mason, can you text Sara so she knows?" I ask.

He picks up his phone and types out a message. "Done."

I head up to my room to change and grab my swimsuit for maybe doing a few laps. I'm not always a big fan of being indoors to work out, but the elliptical is usually decent. I program a cardio work out and set myself up for a "fat burning" session for twenty minutes. It's challenging, and I soon feel much less anxiety and stress from this trip. To help cool off, I quickly change and swim laps for twenty more minutes. I should sleep well, at least.

Wrapping up in a large beach towel, I walk back to my room to find Dillon sitting on the bed, still dressed and watching *Sports Center.*

"You guys didn't stay late," I comment, removing my gym bag from my shoulder and shimmying out of my swimsuit out of his view. Brushing my wet hair, I put my water bottle on the side table.

He shakes his head. "Nah, the guys were pretty beat."

Sitting next to him, I reach for his hand and he gives it to me. Rubbing my knuckles with his thumb, I tell him, "It was a nice wake."

"Thanks." With a big sigh of what seems like regret, he says, "I'm speaking at the funeral tomorrow."

Trying to stay positive, I assure him, "I know you'll do an incredible job."

Looking me in the eyes, he implores, "Do you mind me staying here?

I shake my head. "Not at all. I sleep better with you lying next to me."

We crawl into bed. Dillon is understandably upset, so I slide my arms around his neck and flatten myself against the front of him before tilting my head up and capturing his lips. Quickly our tongues are dancing. Desire rolls through me and he pulls me even closer, deepening the kiss as his body hardens. He untangles himself from me, not breaking eye contact. I watch him stand next to the bed, pulling his shirt over his head and then pushing his pants down. He's standing in front of me in only a pair of colored boxers, the evidence of his desire so clearly displayed before me, making my fingers itch with want.

I slide my fingers across the hard bulge in the front of the soft cotton fabric, enjoying his shudder.

I gasp as his erection is finally revealed. It's big, smooth, and beautiful, and my mouth is watering in anticipation.

He takes a step toward the bed and lets me stroke it up and down a few times, but when I move my lips toward it, he says, "I've wanted you for too long."

I open my towel to reveal my naked body. Dillon visibly sucks in air, and my nipples harden into stiff beads from my desire. He kneels on the bed and spreads my legs wide, my hard nub is swollen with anticipation.

"God, you're beautiful," he murmurs, taking a nipple in his mouth and licking, pulling, and twisting. I moan my appreciation.

His hands explore as he kisses down my taut stomach. When he reaches the top of my pussy, I grab the sides of his face and try to stop him. I've given plenty of blow jobs but never received much in return; I'm not sure how I feel about it.

Taking a deep sniff of my scent, he dips his face down between my legs and licks me from one end of my slit to the other, from top to bottom. His tongue drags across my hard clit, which is so swollen it almost feels like it'll burst. He does it a few times before finally taking it between his lips and sucking it into his mouth. He runs his tongue back and forth across it quickly and I wrap my fingers in his hair, pressing his face into me so hard it's a miracle he can breathe.

My breathing becomes labored, my hips moving involuntarily, and I fist the sheets around me. "I'm going to come!"

He inserts his fingers into my tight canal and thrusts them in and out while his tongue strums my clit. I moan my satisfaction, and even if only for a moment, he looks content.

He wipes his chin of my juices as his other hand reaches across to his wallet on the nightstand, retrieving a condom package. I watch as he rips it open with his teeth and rolls it on.

"Are you ready?" he asks.

I nod, not sure of what to expect. Dillon's much bigger than I've ever had before.

He teases me, rubbing his hard cock over my throbbing clit before entering, moving slowly for a few seconds, giving me time to adjust to his size. Once I'm stretched comfortably around him, he begins to move faster, plunging in and out of me. The look of ecstasy on his face is almost as sexy as the feeling of him inside me.

Each stroke pulls out another level of pleasure until I'm sure I'm going to pass out. He's moaning and panting as he picks up his pace, and I claw at his back, sure to be leaving scratch marks in my wake. I wrap my legs around his body, his hands everywhere as he slams into me repeatedly. He closes his eyes and lifts his chin as he locks in place above me, crying out loudly. I take control of our sex and work him as best I can from beneath him, needing to watch him come undone. He cries out again, and I come from the intense pressure mixed with the deliciously hot sound of him taking what he needs from me.

Limp with exhaustion, we lie here for a few minutes with Dillon resting against me. I run my fingers through his sweat-slicked hair and over his back. I can't help but kiss the side of his face over and over again.

Our limbs are intertwined, our bodies as close as they can be, reassuring ourselves and each other as we fall asleep holding one another.

We both sleep soundly for the first time in weeks.

⸻⊶❦❦⊷⸻

SARA AND I ENJOY THE ZOO while the guys head to the Ford Museum. I haven't spent much time in Michigan before, and I'm surprised by its beauty. It's green and lush, so unlike where I grew up. Denver is high desert, so other than pine and aspen trees, it's dry and brown, though with its own beauty of the purple mountains, the high plains, and the blue sky.

We meet back at the hotel after lunch, then head to the church together for the funeral service. Several friends of Dillon's dad get up and say beautiful things. Siobhan shares several stories and struggles with a prayer, her husband leaving his seat and putting his arm around her to support her and help her finish.

Together they choke out words of wonderful memories and their loss.

When Dillon stands up, he shares stories of his childhood and how his father taught him so many lessons in life. There isn't a dry eye in the house.

Following the service, we all head to Dillon's family home. There are probably fifty people who've joined us, and with the help of my team in San Francisco, I had arranged for a catered dinner for everyone before we left for Detroit.

Dillon is stoic, staying strong for his mom and sister.

I'm looking at the decades of pictures hanging on the walls when a woman comes up and introduces herself. "Hi. I'm Celeste."

Celeste is a curvy platinum bottle-blonde with a lot of shiny makeup. She has the figure of a nineteen-fifties model in a tight black dress, complete with red talon nails that are ready to scratch your eyes out. "Nice to meet you. My name is Emerson." I know exactly who she is, remembering the shower story from the previous night, but not wanting to give anything away and trying to be polite, I ask, "How do you know the Healy family?"

With high confidence, she tells me, "I'm Dillon's girlfriend. We've been dating since high school."

I'm floored by this. Dillon has never mentioned her at all. "Wow. Did you go to Stanford, too?"

"No. I went to school here, and we have a long-distance relationship. I can't leave my mom." She pauses and looks at me carefully before asking, "How serious are you and Dillon?"

I'm quick to assure her, "We're business partners. We aren't dating."

Like a spider trying to lure a bug into her web, she tells me, "He likes you, you know."

I won't fall for her fake charm. "I like him. He's a good business partner and friend."

"Dillon's in California to make money so we can have a big family when he returns to Michigan." She puts a hand on her hip with a cat-who-got-the-canary smile.

I can't think of anything to say, so I squeak out, "Good for you."

She nods at me and walks away.

Sara sidles up to me after Celeste walks away and asks, "Who's that?"

Watching her retreat to the other side of the room with a lot of sway in her hips as she walks, I explain, "Dillon's high school girlfriend warning me to back off."

"What?" Sara asks incredulously.

"Yep. Celeste is marking her territory." I take a big swig of my Irish whiskey.

"What are you going to do about her?"

Trying hard not to show that my feelings are hurt, I share, "Nothing. If Dillon wants to explore a relationship with Celeste, I can't stop him. We're not together. We're just close friends, nothing more."

I'M IN BED READING when my hotel room door opens and Dillon walks in. "I know I didn't call or anything, but I hope you don't mind."

I've been upset about Celeste all evening. I know her idea of what's going on with Dillon is probably not realistic, but I'm still mad. I need to protect myself. Trying not to sound too snotty, I say, "No, I don't mind, but how does Celeste feel about it?"

He stops in his tracks and seems completely surprised by my question. "Celeste?"

I'm letting my anger with her spill over, which is uncool, but I can't stop myself. "She pretty much told me to back off at the funeral today."

Dillon looks like a deer caught in headlights. "Back off from what?"

"You. Celeste shared your history and implied you were picking up where you left off when you make your millions and move home. I'm to get out of the way."

Laughing, he removes his jacket and shoes. "She hasn't been my girlfriend since high school. Ignore her. That's what I do." He moves toward me and holds me tight. "I don't know what I would've done without you here today. Thank you."

Pulling the covers back from me, he sees I'm wearing a pair of boxer shorts and a Stanford golf T-shirt. He climbs on top of me. His kisses are needy, and I respond by moaning into his mouth.

I tug my shirt over my head, and he hands me a condom and presses kisses all over my firm breasts as my nipples harden to his touch. He pushes them together and licks at the nipples in tandem as he growls over and over.

He rubs himself against me and I whimper in response. Lovemaking can come later; I need Dillon to take me hard and fast. Last night was the first in a long time that I'd been intimate, and I need him again.

Pulling my boxers over my hips and throwing them over his shoulder, he smiles as if he's found treasure. "Tell me if you need me to slow down or if I'm hurting you, Emerson." He moves back as I drive against his hard cock pushing against my core.

"Stop talking and start fucking me." I groan as he drives forward, opening me up and working his way into where he belongs, deep inside me.

"You're so damn tight," he grunts.

I mewl and push back, taking more of him. He grips my hips and rocks against me, picking up speed as he grunts softly. Pleasure rolls through me in waves, my shallow breathing increasing as I enjoy the intense pressure of his thickness.

He leans forward and kisses the side of my neck as his fingers slide between the wet folds of my sex. I arch my hips forward and jerk back in rhythm with his deep thrusts as he softly pinches my clit.

"I want to feel you come," he whispers against the damp skin of my neck, and as if he's already gained mastery over my body, it responds to his desire. I let out a guttural cry and come hard, his words commanding and voice thick with passion as I lose myself in it.

"Oh my God," I groan and rock against him, never wanting the moment to end.

DILLON

THE TEAM left this morning. It was nice to have my friends here to support me. I need to find a way to thank them.

Emerson and I made love before she headed out, and I already miss her. The smell of her perfect perfume. The look on her face when she reaches her pinnacle. And I love the look of desire she has when she sees my hard cock. It'll be hard being here without her.

I took care of the hotel room for Emerson, the least I could do for crashing in it. I extended the reservation so I could stay there. The team agreed to allow me to work from here for a few weeks since much of my job can be done remotely as long as I have a computer, internet connection, and my cell phone.

I'm not sure my mom understands why I can't stay with her, but she's trying. She's struggling, and I know she's scared; my dad took care of so much.

Siobhan and Steven are heading home to Texas after helping for the past two weeks, so I spend some quality time with my mom, attempting to get her comfortable with what I can. She's nervous to pay bills, so I set them up to come to me, and I'll make sure they get paid on time. I knew my parents had invested in many of the companies I'd worked for and also several I had personally invested in, so I talk to her advisor, who says she's going to be quite comfortable. They have a good nest egg, which is a significant relief.

Celeste stops by unannounced, and she's a little too friendly. She holds my hand and tells Mom and me that she's going to look out for my mom after I leave. My mom gives a big eye roll behind Celeste's back, and I know I'm in for a big lecture later. I need to have a talk with Celeste, but I don't know where to start. I've told her many times to move on, but she probably thinks that because I'm not married, I'm holding out for her. That is most definitely not the case.

I talk to the team multiple times every day. I'm struggle to keep up with my work, but I'm doing it, slowly but surely. Emerson touches base with me almost every day and shares some sort of tidbit that always makes me smile.

Emerson Winthrop: You missed it. Cameron came in wearing salmon-colored pants, a white dress shirt, and camel-colored suede loafers.

Dillon Healy: He must be in love.

Emerson Winthrop: Agreed!

Emerson Winthrop: John in accounting must have been trying to impress Annabel. He tried to fix the copy machine and is now covered with black toner. I tried to talk him into running home, but he's refusing. Toner everywhere.

Emerson Winthrop: Mason, Cameron, and I ran into Bob Perkins and Terry Klein at a luncheon. Wow. They had girls on both arms and were such assholes.
Dillon Healy: They're douchebags.
Emerson Winthrop: That's exactly what Cameron called them.

I wish I could've been there when they saw Bob and Terry. I know they feel they're smarter than everyone, but Perkins Klein peaked about ten years ago and got too comfortable with how they were investing. They turn down great opportunities, and it's easy to take money from them that they're leaving on the table.

My time with my mom is winding down. When it's time to leave, I tell her that if she needs me, I'll be back right away. She cries as she walks me to the security line at the airport, and I feel incredibly guilty for leaving her.

DILLON

As I HIT THE TARMAC back in San Francisco, I text Emerson.

> Dillon Healy: I'm back.
> Emerson Winthrop: I'm at arrivals. Your chariot home awaits.
> Dillon Healy: You're here?
> Emerson Winthrop: With open arms, waiting for one of your hugs.
> Dillon Healy: See you in a few.

I walk out of security and see Emerson, absolutely radiant in a beautiful pastel green sundress that shows off all her curves. Men all around us are looking at her appreciatively. She has a sign with my name on it, and I walk up and give her a big hug before leaning down and pressing my mouth to her hair, breathing in the sweet smell of her perfume. Her lips are soft when I kiss her, and they open to allow me entry, our tongues dancing a delicate tango.

When we break our kiss, I look down at her and say, "I've missed you."

She smiles at me. "Well, let's get you home. We've missed you."

"We?"

"I should warn you, Molly is in the car and anxious to see you."

I pick up my bag and throw it over my shoulder. "Let's get out of here."

We head to my place and I insist she and Molly come up, the tension between us palatable. I want her, and I know by the way she's fidgeting that she wants me, too.

In the elevator, I move toward her, my cock hard as a baseball bat. It wasn't until I kissed her at the airport that I realized just how much I both want and need her.

Emerson stays with me for the first time at my place. She doesn't put any pressure on me, but I can't hold back.

EMERSON

E HAD AN AMAZING NIGHT of lovemaking. Stealing a look at myself in the closet door mirror and noting my matted hair and raccoon eyes, I quickly detour to the bathroom and attempt to clean myself up.

As I walk into the kitchen, I see him open the fridge and lean over, his black boxer briefs pulling tight on the perfect swell of his ass. My body warms, my cheeks flush, and my stomach contracts. I want him all over again.

When it's just Dillon and me, everything is much easier. I don't need to think about a label for our relationship, or about the future. I can concentrate on him.

He grips the bottom of my dress and pulls it up slowly. I lift my arms and shiver as his fingers brush against my exposed flesh. I'm not an experienced lover, but it's evident that he is. I've never wanted anything as badly as I want him right at this moment.

He tosses my dress aside, and something in his eyes that looks like awe sends jolts through my body. Using the backs of his fingers to trace along my collarbone and the swell of my breasts, he pushes my bra straps off my shoulders and down my arms until my breasts rise up and over the lace, revealing my erect nipples, begging for his touch.

He groans as he lays me down on the bed, and I feel another rush of wetness between my legs. He leans down to run his warm, wet tongue across the sensitive skin above my nipples, and I arch my back off the bed, letting out a groan of my own.

He takes the hint and slowly licks around one of my hard peaks, bringing his other hand up and pinching the other one with his thumb and forefinger. I arch up for more as he finally sucks the other one into his mouth.

Fireworks explode in my brain as he uses his mouth to drive me to the brink of an orgasm without even touching my bare pussy.

I moan his name and he moves his mouth back up to cover mine. While we kiss, I push his shirt off his muscular shoulders and run my hands over the muscles, pressing my bare chest to his.

I can't believe how bold I'm being—I'm usually such a shy and hesitant lover—but something about Dillon set parts of me on fire I hadn't even known existed.

I rub my erect nipples into his firm chest before he goes up on his knees and slides his adept fingers between my legs. He's taking his time, not rushing things, and I'm losing my mind imagining how good he's going to feel once he's buried inside of me.

DILLON

EMERSON IS AMAZING. She somehow has the ability to see me in a way others don't.

To most women, I'm a quick and easy lay. If they make it past one night, they see me as a way to get gifts and expensive dinners.

Our clients see me as someone who can help them become millionaires.

But it's different with Emerson. The way she sees me tells me she could do things with my body that no one else could. That no one ever has.

It's probably a mistake to get involved with her, but I don't care. I want to taste her. All of her. I move lower, trailing kisses down her stomach and across to her hipbone, and she shudders beneath my touch. She's ready again. She wants it as much as I want it, and the realization is the biggest fucking turn-on.

She tastes like honey, and I can't get enough.

I can't remember ever liking someone as much as I like Emerson. I want to know what her favorite candy is, where she likes to read books or shop. She's feisty and passionate, but also gentle, sweet and breakable. I've never thought about any woman the way I think of her. I sometimes wonder what my life would be like without her and my chest hurts at just the thought.

She rolls me on my back and straddles me. Grabbing the condom from the side table, she licks me from the base to the tip, humming as she goes. Rolling the condom on, she climbs on top of me, sliding her wet folds over my length and using her hand to guide me into her. She takes all of me in one slow movement before she pauses, taking the time to adjust to my size. She's wet and hungry for me, and I love it.

Her perfect soft breasts, the pink nipples hard like pencil erasers, beg for my touch as she does most of the work, riding me slowly at first, then faster, up and down before gliding forward and back, climbing a hill of pleasure. Her hand moves around behind me and she strokes my balls, careful to be gentle.

Slowly, I start to thrust with her and guide her hips with my hands as I get harder, moving my thumb to her clit. The pressure on her hard nub each time she moves down on me starts to send her quickly over the edge. Watching the ecstasy cross her face brings me quickly to my climax and I squeeze my eyes shut, the intense waves of my orgasm breaking over me again and again as her pussy milks my cock.

I'm in heaven. And I need to end this relationship. Our work doesn't allow it, and I'm becoming too dependent on her.

EMERSON

Emerson Winthrop: Hey. You up for a run tonight?

Dillon Healy: Sorry, other plans.

Emerson Winthrop: Do I need to schedule time on your calendar to see you?

Dillon Healy: If you'd like. See you tomorrow at the office.

No you won't, and you know that. I'm out of the office all week dealing with our new acquisition, and I haven't seen Dillon in several days. I'm worried about him.

I need to get my mind off him. Maybe I can convince the girls to go out for at least a drink.

I send a group text to CeCe, Greer, and Hadlee: Anyone up for joining me for a drink and maybe dinner tonight?

I immediately receive a yes from all three girls.

Yeah! Now I can think about someone other than Dillon.

WE'RE MEETING AT ONE MARKET, a high-end restaurant facing Treasure Island and the Bay Bridge. I'm the last to arrive and work my way around the table, greeting my three closest friends in The City. I don't know where I would be without these amazing women in my life.

Hadlee stands and gives me a big hug, kissing both cheeks. Her backless black lace dress hits well above her knees atop a very steep pair of Jimmy Choo sandals, her raven hair in a tight pixie cut highlighting her beautiful long neck. She has a brilliant blue pashmina wrap that sets off the sapphire blue in her eyes. "You look beautiful," she tells me.

CeCe's dark pink Prada floral-print velvet midi dress is sleeveless, showing off her tanned and toned arms. Her hair is blown straight, and her makeup is a dramatic smoky eye. "Sweetie," she says as she hugs me, then whispers in my ear, "Fuck 'em."

Always the fashionista of our group, Greer's wearing a silver-gray velvet dress that ties at the waist but has a slit to her hips that shows off her long tanned legs. Her auburn hair is in loose curls and she looks divine. "No hot date with your boyfriend?" Greer asks as she hugs me and kisses me on the cheek.

I take the last open seat and look at my friends. "I hope you weren't waiting too long?"

"Thank you for pulling us together. It seems like it's been ages since we've hung out," Hadlee says.

CeCe calls the waiter over and he makes his way through the throng of people in our noisy restaurant. "What are we drinking, ladies?"

"Bourbon for me," I say.

"I want a Manhattan," Hadlee orders.

"I'll drink a bourbon, too," Greer tells him.

"Are we drinking them straight or over ice?" CeCe asks.

Greer and I both say in unison, "Over ice."

"I guess it's three bourbons over ice and a Manhattan," CeCe recites.

"A round of ice water, too, please," I add.

He disappears and we spend the evening chatting away. We talk about our jobs, the men in our lives, our families, and even touch on politics at one point. It's fun going out with the girls on a school night. We've had little time to go out recently, so this is nice.

I take a Lyft home and call Dillon from the car, but my call goes straight to voice mail. I don't remember him ever being so distant.

◦◦◦◦◦

THE WEEK HAS FLOWN BY, and I haven't talked to him. I don't want to be needy, or high-maintenance. If I didn't work with Dillon, I would guess he's ghosting me. But really, how old are we?

I shoot him a text: Are we golfing tomorrow morning? And I hear nothing back. Crickets.

I share with my therapist how disappointed I am, but she doesn't give me much in response. I let him in, and now he seems to have crushed me. I don't know what to think.

DILLON

I SEE I MISSED another call from Emerson. I can't deal with her right now. I wish she would just stop worrying about me. I'm old enough to worry about myself.

I run into some friends from my early days of living in The City. We drink too much and hang out, debating the stupidest things, like if NASCAR is a sport or if a woman should play professional football. It keeps us busy, and it keeps me out at night and my mind off how much I miss my dad.

When I'm home, I often find myself picking up the phone, wanting to call my dad to share something. It's then that I struggle with his death the most. Occasionally I find company, or I call a friend to keep me company. But it's never Emerson. She wants more from me and honestly, I don't know what I want right now.

Siobhan calls my cell and leaves me a voice mail every day for a week. I can hear her anxiety increasing with each message. Finally, I call her back. I don't want to, but I do anyway. "Hey, sis. What's up?"

With the anger of a momma bear separated from her cubs, she roars, "Where the *fuck* have you been?"

I have a hangover from partying last night, and I don't have the patience for this. "Calm down. What's going on?"

"Mom got Dad's ashes earlier this week. When can you plan on going home to spread them? I don't own the school. I'm just a teacher, so I need to ask for time in advance."

Trying to hold my irritation in check, I reply, "Why do we have to make that decision right away?"

I know she's close to losing it when she explodes, "Are you *kidding* me? Have you talked to mom? She's a *mess*. I'm flying up Friday after school and will spend the weekend with her."

Great, that means I don't have to go and deal with the ashes. Maybe they can spread them without me. "Okay. Let me know if you need anything."

"Are you fucking kidding me? We need *you*, jackass!"

"To do what? I stayed after you left. I'm paying her bills. I talk to her regularly. I don't know what you want from me, Siobhan, but tell me and I'll make sure you get it."

I hear a big sigh over the phone. "Never mind. I'll let you know how it goes with Mom this weekend."

"Great. Have fun," I say to a dead phone line.

God! Everyone wants something from me. Why can't anything be easy? I need to escape to where no one can bother me.

EMERSON

DILLON HASN'T been the same. The loss of a parent must be extremely difficult. He's regularly late for work and often seems hungover, and he missed today's partner meeting entirely. When he finally comes in, he's dressed impeccably in his pressed khaki pants and a blue and white striped shirt. There's not a hair out of place, but when he asks me to meet him in his office, I can smell the whiskey oozing from his pores.

"How are you doing?" I ask. He hasn't returned any of my texts or phone calls, so I wouldn't know.

"Fine." Showing he's all business and not personal, he asks, "How are things going with Accurate?" Before I can answer, he says, "I talked to Bob last night, and he's having problems with the girl working his account."

I'm surprised to hear this from Dillon and not Bob, "Really? He told me last week that he was thrilled with Marie. Let me find out what's going on and I'll follow up with you."

He gives me a dismissal wave. I turn to leave when I hear him say, "If Marie can't get this done, fire her and let's move on."

Stopping in my tracks, I turn back to face him. "Ooookay. We can do that. But what did Bob say, exactly?"

"Emerson, I don't have the patience for this. Do your fucking job. Find out why she has him upset and get it fixed, or we'll fire both of you."

Too stunned to say anything, I simply tell him, "Of course." Then I leave his office, fighting back the tears. I've never seen him like this. I don't know how to handle him right now.

Mason follows right behind me. "What was that all about?"

"He's unhappy with Marie on the Accurate account, and I need to get it taken care of. No worries."

Scrutinizing me, Mason quietly asks so only I can hear, "Are you covering for him, Emerson?"

"No, not at all. I spoke with Bob last week, and he told me all was going well. Apparently last night he told Dillon something else. I need to get it fixed."

Putting his hand on my shoulder, obviously trying to be reassuring, Mason tells me, "I still don't like him barking at you, or anyone else."

"Don't worry about it. Let me see how I can fix it."

I spend the afternoon trying to figure out what's going on, and in the end, Marie is only asking for a lamp for one of Bob's developers. The developer feels it's dark in his office, and with all the coding he's doing, it's making his eyes tired.

I check with Bob and make sure he's happy with Marie, stressing that we can replace her if he'd like. He's quick to tell me that he's thrilled with her and asks that we not make any changes.

"*Emerson!*" I hear yelled from Dillon's office.

I excuse myself from my call and walk down to his office, going no farther than the doorway. "You rang?" Trying to put a smile on my face, I lean against the door jamb in a brown pencil skirt and pressed shirt with the sleeves rolled up to my elbows, a big wide belt, and Louboutin kitten heels.

Dillon's sitting behind his big desk, papers spread everywhere. "What the fuck are you trying to do?"

Not sure what's going on or what needs to be fixed, I remain at the door, just managing to keep my temper in check. "I need more information. What are you referring to?"

His hands are waving around like he's trying to bring a plane into a gate. "I'm looking at this proposal for BetaWorks, and I see you have eight people attached. Are you

trying to bankrupt us? What the fuck?"

Taking a deep breath, I carefully outline why they need four people, which also includes my input. It isn't eight people, and it isn't extravagant. They have an aggressive business plan that will require recruiting help and operational support.

He hasn't listened to one thing I've said. "No. It's not acceptable. They don't need any more than one person from your team. If they can't do the job, we'll find someone who can."

Still standing at his door, I tell him, "I understand you're having a bad day. I'm sorry for whatever I did." Then I turn to return to my own office and take a breath of air.

"Don't you dare walk out on me!" he snarls.

Spinning around and looking at him, I say, "When you're ready to have a reasonable conversation, let me know." With that, I head back to my office, knowing every set of eyes are on me.

"Get back here!" he yells, and I start to turn back to his office.

"Emerson, can you excuse us?" Mason says from behind me. "I need to have a word with Dillon."

"Of course."

Everyone in the office is standing and watching the interaction, not sure what to do. I hold my head up high, push my shoulders back, and despite wanting to cry, I go into my office, shutting the door behind me. I hate the all-glass offices right now. I just want to find a place where I can cry in private.

My assistant knocks on my door and asks, "Emerson, I'm going downstairs to Starbucks. Can I get you anything?"

Grateful for the distraction, I tell her, "If you fly, I'll buy." I smile at the relieved look on her face. "I'd love a venti soy, no-water, no-foam chai," I reach into my purse, pull out my Starbucks card, and hand it to her.

"Great. I'll be right back."

"Thank you." She leaves and I shut the door behind her. Even so, I can still hear Mason and Dillon screaming at one another.

Sara knocks on my door a while later and walks in with my assistant behind her. "Here's your Starbucks card and your chai."

"That was fast. Thank you, Nadine." Turning to Sara, I ask, "So, how are you today?"

"I think my day is going a bit better than yours. How are you?"

Fighting back the tears, I tell her, "I think tonight I'm going for a long run, and then I'm going to drink a bottle of wine all by myself."

"I'm sorry. Dillon's not the same guy he was before his dad passed."

"I think I agree."

As Sara leaves, Mason sticks his head in and asks, "Do you have a minute?"

I'm nervous about this conversation. I could hear the guys talking, though I couldn't be one hundred percent sure what they were saying. But I did hear my name said with a lot of anger. I'm sure Dillon has requested I leave the company.

The knots in my stomach are tight, and I think I want to throw up. "Of course. Sit down."

Looking out at the employees who are milling about and interested in the drama unfolding, Mason asks, "How about we go for a walk?"

Crap! This can't be good.

"Sure." I pick up my chai and grab my coat from the rack.

Mason doesn't say anything until we've cleared the building. "Emerson, tell me what happened with Dillon this afternoon."

I walk through our situation and share my version of what happened, Mason quiet and nodding in the appropriate places as I talk. He asks a few probing questions but doesn't seem to express any opinion one way or the other. I finish with "If you think I should leave, let's work out a plan." And then I hold my breath, because his reply makes or breaks me professionally.

"Emerson, we have no intention of making any changes with you. I agree with you regarding the proposal. I'm not making excuses for Dillon, but this behavior is out of character for him. Please try to let it go. We love you and want you to stay. Our fear is you'll leave us, and we certainly don't want you to."

I want so much to hug him and tell him he made my day. "I know he's been dealing with a lot, so I'll give him some more rope, but at some point, he's going to hang himself."

"I agree. Cameron and I are meeting for dinner tonight. I suppose you and Sara should officially join us, but if you don't mind, the three of us were founders, and we need to figure out our next steps before we make a recommendation to the partners."

"I understand. I can take the yelling as long as we all know it's more Dillon's frustration with his own personal situation and not with me."

He gives me a hug. "Thank you, Emerson. I really needed to hear that."

DILLON IS SITTING ON MY DOORSTEP when I arrive home. Molly is playing with him and enjoying all the attention he's lavishing on her. Traitor.

I'm angry with him. He mistreated me today, embarrassed me in front of people who work for us, and he embarrassed me in front of Mason. Not interested in any apology, I ask, "How did you get into my house?"

"I didn't. Molly was in the backyard and I opened the gate. Can we talk?"

"As long as you're going to be respectful and not yell at me."

He tilts his head to the side, smiles, and says, "I promise. Can we go inside?"

I nod, though I'm nervous to let him in. Once the door is closed behind me, he kisses me deep and hard, aggressive. Much like when he fucks: hot, hard, feral, and at a pace that's difficult to keep up with.

We tear our clothes off and his fingers deftly probe my core, the urgency making me orgasm quickly. We move to the bedroom, and I hand him a condom from the bedside table. He sheaths his erection and I hold on to him, showing how I want him deep inside me.

He dips his tongue past my lips and pushes against my soft core. God, how I've missed the feel of him. I smooth my hands up from his shoulders to find his neck, straining and tight under my fingers. He pulls me toward him, deepening his kiss, pressing my body to his and pushing his hardness against my stomach. I need him in every way, right here and now.

He circles his hips and then pulls his head back. "I'm sorry about today."

"Shush. Fuck me already."

He smiles and his cock pummels my sweet spot, riding me hard. I see the pain on his face, the anguish caused by his father's death.

All of a sudden, it's crystal clear—all the emotions of the day have come crashing down because I'm trying to squash what we have together, what I feel for him. I'm in love with this man. The good-looking man who is above me, inside me.

When he's done, I look up to him getting dressed. "Where are you headed?"

"I have dinner plans. See you tomorrow at work?"

I'm too stunned to even respond. *What the hell just happened? Why did I let him into my home?*

I'm left with the reality of what I am to him. Just another one of his fuck dolls.

I won't be that. I won't let him do that to me and my self-worth.

I SPEND THE REMAINDER OF THE WEEK working on client sites, totally avoiding Dillon. He called last night, and I let it go to voice mail. I don't want to be another name in his little black book, yet somehow that's where I wound up.

Never again.

Saturday night I'm out with the girls. CeCe is aware of what happened with Dillon, both in the office and at my house. She's my champion, actually angrier with him than I am. Loyalty at its finest.

We're meeting at Farallon. I haven't been back since Adam, but CeCe feels it's crucial we have a good experience here. They've reserved us a perfect table, and we order a bottle of champagne.

CeCe raises her glass. "To girl power!"

We all clink our glasses and repeat, "To girl power!"

We have a great dinner and enjoy ourselves. Greer spends the evening telling us all about her recent escapades with her start-up company, which is close to being bought by Microsoft. It's good news for her because she has stock options in the start-up, but also bad news because she won't be part of the sale. Her stories about the antics of the company as they prepare to go big have us laughing until we're crying and our sides hurt.

As we walk out, Greer and Hadlee tell us goodbye and head in one direction while CeCe talks me into going to Quince for drinks in their bar.

"I'll go, but they're a Michelin three-star-rated restaurant with a reservation list months long. Do you think we'll be able to get a place at the bar?"

Pulling at my arm, she starts to walk away. "Let's try. I need to get you out of this funk with Dillon."

Not allowing her to pull me along, I deadpan, "I'm out. Promise. I'm ignoring him—unless it's work-related."

Smiling and facing me, she says, "So now let's talk about how we're going to find you a new guy."

I'm not over Dillon yet. He may have hurt me, but I'm not ready to open myself up again so soon to another man. "I'm off men for a while."

She giggles. "You can't want to go girl, do you?"

I smile. "No. But I love you, sweetheart, and if I were going to become a lesbian, you'd be at the top of the list. I need some time."

We sidle up to the bar and CeCe talks her magic with the bartender. He makes us two Manhattans that we grab immediately. "Damn, these are good!"

I nod enthusiastically. "Absolutely."

Cozying up and positioning herself where she can see every man in the bar, CeCe asks, "What are your plans for the rest of the weekend?"

"I'm playing golf at the Presidio tomorrow morning, and I have a bunch of work to get done." My cell pings, signaling a text. I look at it and see it's Dillon.

Hey.

I'm not planning to respond, but CeCe takes the phone from me and reads the message. "Are you kidding me? Who does he think he is?"

"Ignore it, CeCe. I am."

"So what about your Sunday?" she asks. "I'm headed back to Mom and Dad's. Sure you don't want to join me for Sunday dinner?"

"What time are you going down to Hillsboro?"

"I'll pick you up at your place tomorrow at four."

My phone pings again: What's up?

"Oh, *that* is it!" CeCe tells me. She grabs my phone and responds, Fuck Off.

Before I can stop her, she sends it.

"CeCe! I can take care of myself, and I can certainly handle Dillon."

We're standing at the curb when her car service arrives. I give her a hug goodbye and get in a cab to go home.

As I pull up, I see Dillon sitting on my front porch. Walking past him with my key in hand, I say, "Go home, Dillon."

"Come on, Emerson. You can't be upset with me."

"No. You made it abundantly clear on Tuesday that you just want to be friends with benefits."

"What's wrong with that?"

"I don't want that. I want more. We work together, and *that* is it. Goodbye, Dillon. Go home."

"Please, Emerson. What we have is special. You know I care about you, and I know you care about me."

He definitely isn't the right guy for me. Way too smooth. Way too charming. "Go home, Dillon. I'll see you in the office Monday morning."

Standing, he tries to bring me into an embrace. "Come on, baby. We have so much fun being horizontal."

"Call one of your other 'friends' because we're not *that* kind. We're business associates and friends who *don't* see each other naked."

I push past him and go inside my house alone, leaving him standing there with a look of shock. I guess by his reaction he's never had a woman tell him no once he's put the charm on them.

That's fine. At least I can be a first for him somewhere.

DILLON

I'M CAREFUL, sticking to women who just want or need sex with no strings attached. In a city where straight men are a minority, it's always worked well for me. There are a few women I see semi-regularly, and when I say see, I mean fuck. Elizabeth, who's always dependable when I need to get laid. Tiffany, who lives close and is a fantastic lay. Then there are the two girls I call at the same time. They're sometimes more into each other, but it's fun to participate. San Francisco is incredible if you're a single straight guy.

I thought I might be able to ask Emerson to join my group of friends with benefits, but I don't know what I was thinking. Sleeping with her is amazing, but not good for me personally or professionally.

I have enough going on; I don't need her complication and putting rules in our relationship. Emerson wants more from me than I want to give her. I'm not treating her well, and I don't care. If she intends to be a good girl, I'll take it, but I'm going to show all these narcissist attitudes and take and take and push back when she thinks she has the upper hand.

OUR WORKDAY ENDED, we're all sitting around and drinking beer. Sara runs off to take a call from some guy she's seeing. Cameron and Mason end up with a problem client, leaving Emerson and me.

I want to get drunk tonight. I want to feel numb.

Looking at me, Emerson says, "Don't you think you should slow down?"

"What the fuck do you care?" I snarl.

She winces at my tone. I hurt her. Good. Maybe she'll leave me alone.

She's staring down at her hands when I hear, "Dillon, I care about you. I care a lot about you, and I'm beginning to worry."

I drain my beer and get up, dropping the bottle in the recycling bin before turning to her. "Stop worrying about me."

"I can't help it. You helped me through some dark days, and I only want to help you."

"Why would you want to help me, anyway? We aren't a couple. You were clear that we're business partners who fucked—past tense. Nothing more, Emerson."

Taking a deep breath and biting back tears, she says, "We no longer fuck, but I care. Because I care for you so much it hurts. Because I want to matter to you as much as you matter to me. Because when you shut me out, it gets cold. I get scared."

I can't deal with all this emotion. I walk away, leaving her crying on the couch in the break room.

Why can't anything be easy?

TWENTY-EIGHT

EMERSON

I WASN'T SUPPOSED to fall in love with him, but I have. It's not his fault he doesn't feel the same way. I can obsess over Dillon, or I can let him go.

Mason sent an email to all of the partners, asking for time this afternoon in his office. Something's up. I ask Sara if she knows anything, but she's as concerned as I am and it's pretty clear she doesn't.

In Mason's office, we all look at him expectantly.

Clearing his throat, he says, "Well, I got a call from James over at BingoBongo, and he tells me they've sold 35% of their stock to Perkins Klein."

Dillon jumps up from his chair. "What the hell? James wouldn't be anywhere without us. Emerson moved him to an even stronger position than any of their competitors, and we've been talking to Dell and HP about selling. Perkins Klein's injection will only complicate that."

"Yes, they're taking them to HP. Perkins Klein will manage the negotiations. Emerson, they want you to release your team, and we'll sit out the remainder of the negotiations," Mason explains.

Dillon throws his tablet across the room, smashing it against the wall. "Fuck this! I've worked hours with James. This is not going to happen."

"It's too late. It happened this morning," Mason states.

We all sit stunned by the news. BingoBongo has been a jewel in our crown. We'll still do well with our investment, but we should've done better. Dillon storms out, and we're all left to look at each other.

Cameron finally says, "This is Dillon's fault. His head isn't in the game."

"I don't think that's it," I reply. "We have Emily on-site at BingoBongo, and she would've told us if she knew. Perkins Klein worked this outside."

Mason says, "I agree with Cameron. I think Dillon's eye is not on the ball. We've lost six recent acquisitions, and now we're losing actual clients, all to Perkins Klein. We need to consider that this may no longer be a good home for Dillon."

Sara looks like she's going to cry. "How can you hang this on Dillon? We're getting big, and there are too many balls in the air."

"BingoBongo is in his portfolio, so it's his responsibility, Sara," Mason tells her without condescension in his voice.

Trying to reason with Mason and Cameron, I implore, "He helped found this company. His behavior seems off because he's taking his dad's death hard."

"You're making excuses for him, Emerson. I think we need to have a serious conversation about the possibility of change," Cameron replies.

Mason says, "Over the past year, we've missed six companies in our sweet spot that should've been sure things. We're now seeing an exit of our current client base, which erodes at our initial investments."

"I want to think about all this information tonight. I'd like all of us to meet for breakfast tomorrow morning at Benny's in Capitol Hill. I know this goes without saying, but Sara and Emerson, please don't say anything to Dillon," Cameron states.

I slowly walk back to my office, stunned by this turn of events. I know I'm not happy with Dillon, but this is his company. How can we do this to him?

I CAN'T SLEEP with my brain going a thousand different directions. I have a missed call from Dillon, but he didn't leave a message, so I'm not calling him back. This whole situation brings me so much anxiety that I get up early and hit four buckets of golf balls at the driving range to work out some of my frustrations, then shower at home before meeting the team for breakfast.

After everyone's seated, Sara asks, "Well, after a night of rest—if you were able to get any rest because I sure wasn't—what are everyone's thoughts?"

"Well, I ran through the numbers," Cameron starts. "Dillon's mistakes have cost the company over a billion dollars in missed revenue. It means we limit our growth and our bonuses are looking to be thirty-six percent less. I think it may be time to look at someone else."

"No one in Silicon Valley understands the numbers like Dillon does," I retort. "I'll go with whatever we decide as a group. However, I have to believe we need to push him for a leave of absence and insist that when he comes back, he needs to be fully back. It means he needs to be sober, and we won't tolerate any kind of outbursts we've witnessed these past few weeks."

"I agree for a forced leave of absence with a meeting in three or six months with us," Sara says. "It'll give him the time he needs to figure out what he wants to do and if he wants to return, he needs to make his case to us on why he wants to stay. Then we make the decision on our next step. It'll allow us to save his reputation but also gives us the opportunity to casually look for a new numbers guy."

Before Mason makes his decision known, our breakfast arrives and we're all sitting and eating quietly. Mason finally says, "I agree with Cameron that it may be time for Dillon to leave our ranks, but I do like Emerson and Sara's suggestion of the forced leave and then a meeting on what we all want and need. Cameron, can you buy off on a leave of absence?"

"How long are you thinking? Three months or six?" Cameron asks.

"I'd like six. What do you all think?" Mason asks.

We all agree. None of us has much of an appetite to eat our breakfasts. Sara will reach out to the attorneys and get it all set up with them. They'll be in tomorrow morning to meet with Dillon and us.

As we're walking out the door, I can't help but think the gray skies of San Francisco weigh down on us and our decision.

Mason asks, "Emerson, do you have a minute?"

"Of course."

"I know you and Dillon have become rather close in the year and a half you've been with us. Please try not to say anything to him."

I stop and turn to him. "Mason, I love all of you as my family. It's hard for me to see this happening, but I know he's hurting, and it's what is best for him and for the company. It'll be good for him to spend some time considering his options. I'm comfortable with our decision, and I promise not to tell him anything."

THE NEXT MORNING, the four of us and two of our outside counsel are in the conference room waiting for Dillon to arrive. He's over an hour late. As soon as he walks in, I can smell the whiskey and know he's ready for a fight.

Looking at the people gathered around the conference room table, he demands, "What the fuck is this?"

Our lead counsel sits and says, "Dillon, the partners are concerned about you and your decision-making abilities."

Dillon's eyes are bloodshot and puffy. "You can't touch me. I'm a founder of this company, and I'm an owner," he roars as he pounds the table with his fist.

Mason steps in and pushes a copy of his contract across the table toward him. "Under paragraph 22, section C, we have the ability to exercise a six-month notice when there's cause. Dillon, the loss of six of your clients from your portfolio, your sobriety, and your anger all meet the definition of cause."

"Dillon, the partners feel that with all that's happened in your life, you need a break," the lawyer explains. "The preference is for you to figure out if you want to remain here at SHN. We'll pay your base salary for the next six months, and you're not eligible for any bonuses during your leave. We'll agree to a date to meet again after the six months are up, and we can see where things are at."

"No fucking way!" Dillon yells.

As was discussed before the meeting, Sarah and I get up and walk out, leaving it up to the lawyers, Cameron, and Mason.

Dillon looks at me as I stand, and I can see the hurt this is causing him. He knows he's hurt me, but I don't hold it against him here. This is business, not personal.

DILLON

I'M IN COMPLETE SHOCK. I thought these people were my friends. I can't believe they blame me for the loss of business this year. My numbers are solid, I know it. There's something wrong here. I don't know how Perkins Klein is doing it, but they're undercutting our numbers to take business and money from us.

This is the company I helped found, and damn it, I'm angry. Rather than make a scene, I chose to sit here and look through the documents that were given to me. I have six months to figure out what my next steps are going to be.

I no longer listen to what anyone is saying. The lawyers ask for a signature, and I sign. I ask them to send a copy to my home along with my personal items, and then I get up and leave, out the front door and across the street into a bar. It's early, but they should be open.

As I look around, the morning drinkers are being held up by the bar and not the other way around. An older woman stares down at her light golden drink. Her hair is platinum blonde, her breasts barely held back by the buttons of her white blouse. Her brown wool skirt is tight. She might've been considered beautiful once.

She looks at me and nods. I nod back. I notice she doesn't have a wedding ring on her left hand, but she has plenty of jewelry. I ask, "Can I buy you a drink?"

"Sure. Whatever you're having." She leans in and I can smell her perfume. It's sweet, fruity with a hint of lavender. "My name's Noreen. What's your name?"

"Nice to meet you, Noreen. My name is Dillon." Our drinks arrive and we finish quickly, then order a second and third round. Noreen is progressively friendlier as the booze keeps coming. I excuse myself for the bathroom, and when I come out, she's leaning against the wall with her ankles crossed in front of her.

I lean forward and she puts her arms around my neck. Sliding my hand over the curve of her ass, I squeeze tightly as I explore her mouth fully. She takes every bit of what I'm giving and meets me with a hot passion that leaves me hard and wanting.

She gets down on her knees and opens my pants. I'm leaning against the wood-paneled wall as she takes my engorged cock into her mouth. I groan and look down at her as she continues to suck me, licking my lips. Watching me intensely, she lets moans roll out of her mouth and sucks me harder. I hold the sides of her head while I push deeper and deeper, hitting the back of her throat. She moves one hand to stroke my sack, and my eyes roll back in my head as my mouth drops open.

"I'm going to come."

But she doesn't stop. The image of Emerson with her pretty pink lips around my cock races through my mind and I steel my resolve. I don't need to relive her pleasuring me with Noreen on her knees in front of me. I send my seed deep down her throat.

Standing, Noreen wipes her chin and tells me, "My turn next."

I watch her leave, then pull my pants up and walk out the front door of the bar.

I meet up with a bunch of friends from Stanford at another bar and get blackout drunk. I wake up in some girl's apartment with no idea who she is or any memory of our night.

I'm becoming a vampire. I sleep all day and am up all night, drinking and sleeping with various women I meet. I don't care if they're young, old, black, white, thin, or fat; I pound the shit out of them and get my rocks off. I've become a Class-A jackass.

I SEE SIX MISSED CALLS from Emerson. I can't talk to her. I need a break, and I feel completely betrayed by the partners—her in particular.

When I wake up, I can hear someone in my place moving around. I see a large glass of water next to my bed and a bottle of ibuprofen. I don't remember putting it there.

Pulling on a pair of pants, I wander into the living room to see who's here and am surprised and pissed to find it's Emerson. She looks surprised to see me conscious.

"Who the fuck let you in?" I growl.

Standing defiantly in black yoga pants and a Star Wars T-shirt, a black garbage bag half-full of pizza boxes and bottles in one hand, she wipes a wisp of hair from her eyes with the other and then puts it on her hips. "I did. I still have your key. You haven't responded to any of my voice mails or texts."

"Well, obviously I didn't want to talk to you."

"Your house is a wreck, and it smells of sex, stale pizza, and Irish whiskey."

"Just leave, Emerson. You fucked me over, and I have absolutely nothing to say to you."

"I was not behind your departure from SHN." She drops the trash bag and puts both hands on her hips. "Use this sabbatical. Take this time to figure out if you want to be with us at SHN. We want and need you back, but we need you sober and without crazy outbursts. And I want my friend back. I don't want to sleep with you ever again, but I want the kind man back who pulled me out of the darkest hole I've ever been in."

Exasperated, I tell her, "Just leave, Emerson."

I can see tears forming as she nods. She hands me my house key and walks out the door.

Good riddance. I don't need Emerson in my life. She's a complication and a distraction.

THIRTY

EMERSON

I WASN'T *supposed to fall in love with him. I wasn't supposed to need him. I wasn't supposed to want him. But I did fall in love with him, I do need him, and I most certainly want him.*

I've gone from angry to hurt and back to angry. I know I shouldn't be in love with Dillon, but I am. Work is improving, but we all agree it isn't the same without him.

CeCe talks me into joining her and friends for a night out. Clubbing isn't typically my thing, but I relent.

I decide on a short black leather dress with black leather high-heeled boots to my knees, and I've flat-ironed my hair so it's straight. My makeup is dark, and my lips are bloodred. I may not want to be at the club, but I look like I belong.

Dillon spots me before I see him. When I notice him staring at me, my stomach drops. I'm not sure if I can speak with him. I don't know what to do. Do I go up to him and talk to him, or ignore him?

My internal debate continues, and I watch him cross to the bar. CeCe sees him and beelines it over to him. I follow, but I'm not fast enough. "How fucking dare you! Emerson has been nothing but supportive of you and all your shit. It's because of you that she met Adam, and now you're blaming her for *your* inabilities?"

She pushes her pointer finger in his chest. "You know, the partners were pushing to release you. It's because of Emerson that you have a paid sabbatical. You can show everyone you want your job despite the fact that you're drinking yourself to death while you bed half the women in San Francisco and hurt my best friend. Get it together, asshole, and leave Emerson alone!"

His mouth is hanging open, apparently shocked by CeCe's dressing down. She turns on her heels and storms off with a look of satisfaction. All the people in earshot of the tirade are staring. The women glare at him with disgust; the men have looks of pity. Dillon doesn't seem to know what to do. He throws a twenty on the bar and leaves without his drink.

CeCe is proud of her moment, and I'm embarrassed. Not because she went to town on him because of me, but because it's another reminder of our feelings not matching. I love him, and he only loves himself.

I wait about a half hour, then excuse myself and head home.

DILLON

*I*T COULD BE MONDAY, Thursday, or Saturday. I don't know, and I'm not sure I care. I have no real memories from last night beyond going out with some new friends and drinking Irish whiskey. I don't know how much time I lost in the darkness, or what took place.

As I come out of the fog, I see that I'm on my bed. The lights are low. Sheets are wrapped around my ankles, soft and cool against my skin. Some girl I've never seen before is on top of me and we're having sex.

How did I get here?

Wait. Can this be right? I'm having sex, and I've never seen her before. It's as if the universe dropped me into someone else's body. But I seem to be enjoying it. I'm making all the right sounds, at least.

She collapses beside me and weaves her legs through mine. I wonder if I should be worried right now, but I'm not scared.

The girl is cute and has an okay figure. "You really know how to wear a girl out," she says, breathing hard. It seems unfair that she should know me and I don't know her, but I'm unsure of how to ask her name.

"I should go," she tells me as she snuggles in closer.

I don't know what to say, so I stay with the stranger in the shadows of my bedroom, looking out onto The City. As she lies in the crook of my arm, I have so many questions, the loudest of which is *How did I get home?*

I sleep, though not soundly. Someone's pounding on my front door. My building has a doorman; how did anyone get up?

Glancing at my bedside clock, I see it's after ten. There's daylight, so I guess it's morning. I leave the woman in my bed and walk to the front door.

Mason's face is strained, and I can tell he's angry, but I don't give a fuck. "What do you want?" I demand.

"It's about time you answered the door."

Turning the television to *Sports Center* and grabbing a bottle of water from my fridge, I walk by him and sit on the couch. "I'm busy. Go away."

He fists his hands at his sides until they're white. "Are you going to waste your leave getting blackout drunk?"

"What do you care? Go home, Mason. Leave me alone."

"Dillon, you're my best friend. We want you back at the office. We need you. Everything's going to shit."

"I already know you and Cameron wanted me gone. It was the girls who talked you into the leave. Go the fuck away."

"You're right. Emerson and Sarah came up with the idea of the leave, but it didn't take a lot of talking us into offering the time off to you. Pull your head out of your ass. I know losing your dad sucks—I lost mine when I was seventeen—but you've got to pull it together. You're going to lose your business, and some people—Cameron, Sara, Emerson, and me—may not be here for you if you can't figure it out. Grow the fuck up. Get it together!" Then he turns and storms out of my apartment, slamming the door behind him.

I stare at the television and replay the conversation in my head. *I don't fucking need him or any of them.*

I hear the strange woman clear her throat. She's dressed now and heading toward the door. "Well, it sounds like you're busy. Thanks for last night. It was a lot of fun. I hope to see you later. You've got my number."

I wave goodbye, not even looking at her. I'm still angry with the way Mason spoke to me. I know he's right, but fuck him. I don't need him.

I'm out of liquor. I call to have some whiskey delivered. *My head hurts. I need a nap.*

I fall asleep on the couch. The doorman rings my apartment and informs me that he has a delivery from the liquor store and a box the postman delivered for me. He brings them up to my apartment.

The box is from my mom. I've been ignoring her calls. I'm such a shitty son. Pouring myself a tall glass of whiskey, I sit down to open the package.

I'm not sure I want to know what she sent. I finish my second whiskey before I relent and finally open it. Inside the box looks like little gifts, small packages carefully wrapped in white tissue paper. Unwrapping one item at a time, my heart hurts as I look at what she sent me: my dad's college class ring from the University of Michigan; a picture of my parents taken when I was in high school in a delicate silver frame; a pocket watch that had belonged to my great-grandfather, my grandfather, my dad, and now I guess to me. There is a picture at a Stanford football game of me and my dad—me in my football uniform, him dressed in a winter coat and scarf, obviously handled a lot based on the frayed edges. There are a few other small wrapped items, but once I see my mom included my grandmother's engagement ring, I lose interest in the remaining packages. I stop and stare at the ring.

I realize the only woman I have ever considered making any commitment with is Emerson, and I've fucked that up royally. She hates me, as she should. I've entirely alienated her. If I weren't such an asshole, I would've realized I'm completely, utterly, and irrevocably in love with Emerson.

I feel alone. I miss my dad. I miss my friends. And I miss Emerson.

I finish my whiskey and call two old friends, Brittney and Champagne. They're always up for a good time, and what better way to get over a girl than to get under two at the same time.

I CONSIDER LETTING my ringing phone go to voice mail, but it's my mom. I might as well talk to her.

"Hey, Mom. I got your package. Thanks."

"I tried to tell you it was coming, but you're so busy. How are you doing?"

I have an internal debate, then decide I might as well tell her the truth. "Things aren't going well at work right now, and my personal life is a wreck. I'm a mess, and I can't blame it on anyone but myself."

"I received a call from Mason. He tells me they're worried about you."

Running my hands through my greasy hair, I fight back tears. "I'm sorry they had to do that."

She says softly, "We're all worried about you, sweetie. Why don't you come home for a few weeks? I need you, and I think you need me. Maybe we can manage our grief together?"

I cry into the phone. "I miss Dad so much... and I've fucked everything up so bad."

"I miss him, too. Come home, sweetheart. We can figure out how to fix this."

We talk for a bit longer, and I book my flight home for tomorrow. Going home will be good for me, I'm sure.

EMERSON

*I*T'S SHORTLY AFTER SIX O'CLOCK in the morning, and I'm hitting a bucket of golf balls at the driving range. With each shot, the pressure between my shoulder blades releases a tiny bit. The temperature is cool but at least dry, and with the constant motion, I'm breaking a sweat.

The golf pro approaches. "I haven't seen you in a while, Emerson. I thought maybe you'd fallen in love."

I stop to smile at him, welcoming the short break. "No. I sold my company to a VC firm here in The City and my time isn't always my own anymore."

"Good to see you back. You still have the best swing around here." He waves as he goes to greet his lesson.

I'm in the mood to play a round this weekend. At least eighteen holes. I wonder if I can talk Dillon into a game. As I'm thinking of how to ask, my cell phone pings, indicating a text. It's from Dillon. I'm going home to Michigan today for a few months. If you wouldn't mind, please grab my mail about once a week and check on my place. I'll leave a key in an envelope with my doorman. Thx.

I text him back, No problem. Call me if you ever want to talk. I miss you.

He never responds. I want to call him, to hear his voice, his laugh. I want to feel him close to me, but if I do, I know I'll never get over him. My superpower is the ability to locate the most obvious asshole wherever I go and attract him to me. It's a gift. Now if I could figure out how to not fall for them once they came close.

After finishing my bucket of golf balls, I cry as I drive home. I keep thinking we revealed new and hidden parts of ourselves over the past few months. We lay exposed and vulnerable to one another, not something we do with others easily, I'm sure. I need time to recover and recuperate before I can move on. Repairing a broken heart is never easy.

DILLON

*M*Y FLIGHT HOME IS UNEVENTFUL—as it should be.
Randomly on the plane, I text Celeste to let her know
I'm coming to town. It feeds my ego that she's interested in me
and what I'm doing. We talk about once a month, and it was nice
that she came to my dad's wake and funeral. I feel like I should
see her while I'm visiting. I don't want to screw her; I just want
to spend time with someone who likes me for me.

As I get off the plane and clear security, I see my mom in a
pair of light pink capris and a white collared shirt with a lime
green belt and matching lime green shoes. She always looks put
together. The only problem is she appears much frailer than
when I left three months ago.

Her smile is all teeth when she sees me. I swoop her into my
arms and twirl her around like a schoolgirl. "I've missed you," I tell
her.

"I've missed you, too." After I put her down and we begin the
walk to the car, she asks, "How long are you here for?"

"Well, the company put me on paid leave for the next five months. I may not stay the entire break, but I'm here as long as you need me."

She gives me a reassuring hug. "You're welcome to stay as long as you want."

She hands me the keys, and I drive us home. It's a beautiful spring day, and I love the look on the locals' faces, like they're coming out of their dark winter cocoons and seeing sunshine for the first time in months.

We spend what's left of the afternoon together, though being in the house is difficult for me. It reminds me of my dad and how I let him down.

My mom must sense my trepidation but is clearly excited that I'm here. She makes my favorite meal—her homemade version of Hamburger Helper. It's horrible for you, but it tastes good and reminds me of my childhood. It's straightforward—ground beef browned and crumbled, then add two cans of condensed tomato soup, a can of tomato sauce, and half a stick of butter. Bring to a light simmer and pour over a pound of cooked elbow noodles. I'm eating well tonight.

My mom asks me if I want to play some rummy, but I decline. "I'm going to meet up with a few friends at Harry's Bar."

She pats me on the arm. "Just don't be too late."

I know meeting Celeste is going to be a mistake. And I know if I tell my mom I'm going to meet her, she'll be disappointed. I don't want to go, but I don't want to stay here either.

The dark bar smells like old cigarette smoke, and the neon signs covering the walls cast more light than lamps do. It looks the same as it did when we weren't old enough to drink but they served us anyway.

I sit on a brown pleather barstool and order a whiskey. Celeste comes in and I give her a sexy smile, my eyes roaming down her taunt, tan flesh, imagining all the ways I could make her moan. She's breathtaking, and yet a dime a dozen. Her red blouse is see-through, and her short black leather mini skirt is more of a micro skirt. As she climbs on the barstool, I see she isn't wearing underwear. *I'm not going to sleep with her.*

The bartender approaches and says, "Celeste, good to see you. White wine spritzer?"

She's rubbing my thigh, inching closer and closer to my cock as she flirts back with the bartender. "Tom, you know me so well."

Tom delivers a new drink for me and Celeste's white wine spritzer. She hands me my whiskey before leaning back and closing her eyes. "I've missed you."

I don't know how to respond. Celeste puts her focus on me, watching me intently. I know she wants me to tell her I've missed her, too, but I can't bring myself to lie to her. I smile and pick up my drink, taking a deep pull. I've been here ten minutes and already I've had two double shots.

The conversation is stilted. Celeste is trying too hard, and I'm not making it easy; I'm only here because I don't want to be at home. She wants something I don't, and rather than be a man and tell her, I'm a jerk and hope she gets the hint.

Two drinks later, she walks me to my car.

"Are you sure you can drive?" she asks.

I'm entirely too drunk to drive, but I don't want to go home with Celeste, and I certainly don't want her to come home with me. "Look, I'm staying with my mom. You know how she is. There's no way you can come home with me. I'll just sleep it off here in my car."

Shimmying up to me, she pins me against the car. I feel the heat of her body as she leans flush to me, her lips searching for mine. I slide my hand over the curve of her ass and squeeze tightly as I explore her mouth thoroughly. Desire rolls through me, deepening the kiss as my body hardens.

When she gets down on her knees, I whisper, "No...," but I can't seem to stop her. She unbuckles my pants and takes my thick cock into her hands, stroking me with one hand and then the other in a slow, tight fashion. My teeth sink into my bottom lip and I close my eyes, dropping my head back. Hoarsely, I whisper, "God, that feels good."

"Mmmm... looks good." She moves up and rolls her tongue across my thick head before taking me in her mouth. My breath catches in my chest and I groan, lifting my hips and forcing more of my cock deep down her throat. I come hard, and she takes her time drinking it all down and licking me clean.

Standing and wiping her chin, she says, "That's a reminder of what you've been missing. When you're ready to come home, we'll marry and start our family. I promise you can have one every night."

She gets up and sashays to her car across the dimly lit parking lot. I turn to look back down the road as she walks away, honestly not caring. Taking a seat in my car, I relive what just happened. I can't see her again.

I finally feel like I can drive home and pour myself into bed about 4:00 a.m. still probably drunk, definitely exhausted and alone.

I FEEL AS IF I'VE JUST LAID DOWN when my mom comes in, turns the lights on, opens the curtains, and shakes me awake. Rolling over, I look at the clock and see it's almost nine. In her "don't mess with me" voice, she demands I meet her downstairs. As she's shutting the door, she says, "Fifteen minutes or I'm going to get nasty."

Uninterested in finding out step two of her wake-up call, I slowly sit up. My head is killing me and my stomach flip-flops. Finding a pair of sweatpants and a Stanford football T-shirt, I dress as quickly as I can. I can smell the coffee brewing.

As I walk into the kitchen, she offers me bacon, scrambled eggs, and toast.

Sitting across from me at the table, she holds her cup of coffee with two hands and looks at me. I can tell she isn't happy.

Typical of my mom, she's direct. "What happened in San Francisco?"

I'm not ready to talk about it. I already feel like a failure, and I'm not prepared to tell my mom about everything that happened. But she isn't having any of that, so I give up and begin sharing the story of my demise. As I talk, I may embellish a few of the details and leave a few things out, but I make sure she knows I'm the victim in this mess.

As I talk, she nods when she's supposed to and asks lots of questions. I'm sure she's figured out that I'm not the victim. My sister always said Mom had the best bullshit meter.

"And what about that pretty girl, Emerson? From what I could tell, she was very much in love with you."

"I don't think so. We have a non-fraternization clause in our partnership agreement. We can't get involved with each other."

"I know that, as your mother, I'm supposed to believe you don't sleep with women, but I know you spent every night with her when she was here at the Townsend." I look at my mom in wonder. *How did she know I didn't stay in my own room?* "So what happened?"

To further emphasize that I'm a victim in this mess, I share, "She didn't back me up. She told a BS story about supporting this leave rather than an outright firing. And her friend went out of her way to embarrass me about it when she felt I was stalking Emerson."

"You don't believe she supported your leave? Why?"

Feeling boxed in and humbled, I confess, "Because I wasn't very nice to her."

Sitting back in her chair, she takes a sip of her hot coffee. "Ahhh. I see. I think if I were you, I would believe Emerson defended you." She lets it sink in for a moment while I eat my breakfast. When I think she's done with her lecture, she asks, "And last night? Where were you?"

I let out an exasperated sigh. "Out with friends."

"Celeste?"

"Maybe."

"You're an adult. You have a beautiful and smart woman in San Francisco. I'm not going to tell you Celeste isn't for you, but be careful. That girl has been pining for you since high school. If you want to marry her, I'll happily love her as my daughter-in-law."

"Mom, I promise I'm not going to marry Celeste."

"Then you need to tell her that. Your Aunt Ginny overheard her tell Emerson at the wake to back off." She waves her finger at me. "She has her eyes set on you, and she wants you. Leading her on isn't fair to her. I love you, but I raised you better than that."

"I hear you."

"Now, it sounds like you're going to be here for a while. Why don't you get into the shower? I'll have a list of things you need to do while you're here."

I wasn't expecting to work while visiting with my mom, thinking we might just hang out, so I'm shocked. "What?"

Getting up from the table, she rinses her coffee cup and puts it in the dishwasher. "This isn't a free ride. I need you to do a few things your dad would normally do."

I reluctantly get into the shower, the warm water spraying my face and body, relaxing it a small bit at a time. Telling my mom about what happened helps.

In that moment, I realize I've managed my life all wrong. I keep replaying what my mom said. San Francisco has turned me into an asshole.

As I return to my childhood bedroom, sitting on my bed, I see a list of about twenty chores that need to be done around the house: painting, planting, weeding, plant and furniture removal. It's a lot of everything.

She suggests we start with removing all the juniper bushes in her front gardens. The huge shrubs have been here as long as

I can remember. It takes me an entire day to cut the bush down to a stump, and then another day to dig out the root ball. There are over a dozen she wants removed.

As I analyze and think through everything that's happened, I realize I don't like the jerk I've become. I miss my friends and my work. I decide I'm going to use this time to get myself together. First on the list: no more Celeste.

EACH TUESDAY LIKE CLOCKWORK I receive a package from home. I swear each time I open the envelope I can smell Emerson's perfume—spicy vanilla with a hint of carnations, maybe? She always includes a note. Most tell me she misses me. I want to call her, but I don't know what to say.

I fucked up bad.

EMERSON

WITH THE DISTANCE, I have more clarity. Dillon is the person who helped me through the darkest time in my life. He's my rock, my friend, and my business partner. He's also a man. I grew up with four brothers, so I know they don't talk easily about their feelings, but I'll be here for him if and when he's ready or needs me.

Molly and I make it part of our routine to walk to his house every few days and pick up his mail. He gets a lot of junk mail. I bring the bills into the office and once a week overnight them to him at his mom's. It's my only contact with him. I include a note each week making sure he knows I'm here.

I'M BACK TO TAKING MUNI to and from work every day. I miss riding with Dillon, but I do enjoy the solitude the bus provides. It's the only time I have to read anymore. I've been reading these wonderful romance suspense novels. Comparing my life to the characters in my book, I wish it were as easy. Why does love need to be so much work?

When I arrive at the office, my assistant meets me at the door with a chai tea in hand. This isn't good. "What's wrong?" I ask.

"Mason's on a rampage. The partners have a meeting in fifteen minutes in his office."

I can feel the bile rising in my stomach. Giving my assistant a weak smile, I thank her and boot up my computer to do a quick cursory check of my email for anything that needs to be handled immediately. I forward a half-dozen emails to various members of my team and to my assistant. At least those fires have been pushed back and are at bay. For the moment.

Gathering my leather composition book, a pen, and my tea, I walk down to Mason's office. My feet feel like they're encased in concrete with each step. I'm not sure I can manage any more bad news.

Sara comes rushing in, her coat and briefcase in hand. She's usually turning the lights on in the morning, but I think she's like me, overwhelmed and struggling to keep up.

Joining the partners meeting is Vice President of Finance, Tim Watt. He was trained by Dillon and is under enormous pressure from the partners, and it's beginning to show. In a pair of gray dress pants and a light green pressed shirt with the shirtsleeves rolled up, he's perspiring profusely and is obviously nervous.

Mason begins the meeting by thanking everyone for coming. I can hear the stress in his voice. He turns to a whiteboard and points to a list of four companies I've never heard of. "Perkins Klein announced this morning that they had invested almost five million dollars in each of these companies."

We're all speechless. I sit back in my chair and let out a breath I hadn't realized I was holding.

Cameron asks Tim, "Why didn't the financial teams see this and help us approach them? This is our sweet spot."

Tim stutters, "W-we're fielding over a thousand requests a day. I'll have to check, b-but the names aren't familiar, and I'm not sure they approached us for funding."

Mason can only shake his head, clearly not happy with the answer. "Tim, go check with your team and find out." Tim nods and practically runs out the door. Mason continues, "To make matters worse, we were outbid on another round with Tim Connor's new venture."

Sara sits back in her seat. "Shiiiiit. Does anyone else see a pattern here?"

Cameron nods. "You've read my mind. Perkins Klein is gunning for our business. Looks like we may have a mole."

We all lament the companies, and Cameron makes a solid argument about espionage that's hard to ignore.

Sara shares, "A few weeks ago, presented with this argument, I would've thought Dillon was our spy. Not on purpose, but maybe in a drunken stupor where he might've had some pillow talk. I don't believe it now. We need to figure out who it could be."

A knock sounds at Mason's office door, and we see Tim through the glass. Holding a spreadsheet, he goes through all four names. They all approached us the week after Dillon left. We had face-to-face meetings with each of them and requested additional information we never received. All four were considered "strong buys," which means we wanted them in our portfolio, but they were in preliminary stages, and Perkins Klein has already funded them.

This is beginning to scream corporate espionage. We have a big problem.

Sara asks, "Tim, can you get with your team and find out where the information went and why it wasn't followed up on?"

He nods and leaves the room.

Cameron sits back, staring out the window at the Bay Bridge and a large tanker floating underneath. "I agree with you, Sara. We can't blame this on Dillon. We have a mole. But the question is how do we ferret them out? And more importantly, how do we make Perkins Klein pay for what they've done?"

DILLON

I SEE MY CELL PHONE RINGING. It's Celeste. I look at it and have an internal debate on whether or not to answer it. I'm weak. "Hello."

"Hey there, big guy. How about we grab a pizza from your favorite spot and hang out at my house and see what happens?"

I know it's not a good idea, but I agree. "Sure. You can get pizza from wherever. I can be there about seven."

"Perfect. I'll see you then," she breathes.

"Bye." Looking around, I see my mom standing there. "Eavesdrop much?"

"I guess you have dinner plans with Celeste?"

"Yep. I don't want a lecture, Mom."

"I'm not giving any lectures. I already told you my thoughts."

Getting up from the table, I tell her, "I heard what you said. I haven't decided what to do."

WHEN I ARRIVE AT CELESTE'S HOUSE, she opens the door wearing only a short pink satin robe. Her nipples are erect and begging to be pinched, sucked, and handled. She looks good, but she isn't Emerson.

We sit in the living room and she gets on her knees, unzipping my pants.

"It's been a rough day," I tell her.

She laughs as she pulls out my soft cock, her lower lip stuck out in a pout as she starts stroking me. "What, not happy to see me?" She tugs harder on my shaft. "It's gonna get rougher."

"We shouldn't," I tell her, but I'm not forceful and she doesn't stop. I gently touch Celeste, halting her assault on my flaccid member.

She pouts as she glides her mouth over me, her tongue edging around the rim of my cock. It feels good—she always feels good—and I'm relieved when I start to harden.

Feral grunts escape me as I thrust into her throat, but my mind is on Emerson. I'm envisioning myself pulsing into Emerson's mouth as I hold her head and start quickening my pace.

I need this ache to end, and I know Emerson is the only one to do it. My longing for her increases as her unique mixture of tenderness and strength goes into every touch.

I shoot my load deep down Celeste's throat, and she chokes and runs to the bathroom.

I shouldn't be here. I need to go home. My mom is right—I'm still a jerk.

Sitting on Celeste's couch, I close my eyes and all I can see is my mom. The look when she told me I needed to be fair to Celeste. Waves of guilt rock through me like the tide crashing on the beach.

When Celeste returns from the bathroom, I ask her, "Celeste, we were great once, weren't we?"

She looks confused. "We still are great."

"Why do you think we're still great?"

"Because despite the distance, we still love one another."

I take a deep breath. "I understand you met my friend Emerson at my dad's services."

Her eyes cloud over, and I see the green monster of jealousy in her eyes. Very clipped and strained, she says, "I did. She's a skank."

With my elbows resting on my knees, I put my face in my hands. "Actually, Emerson isn't a skank. She's been a friend to me despite my not deserving it. I haven't treated her well."

"What are you trying to say, Dillon? We agreed when we were fourteen years old that we would get married one day. I've been waiting for you to get your act together and grow up."

"I love her, Celeste. I'm here in Michigan sobering up and pulling my life together so I can get Emerson back."

"You're a fucking asshole!" she yells. "I can't believe after all this time, you're telling me to get lost now. I've given you the best years of my life."

"I didn't ask you to, Celeste. I've even encouraged you to date other guys."

"Fuck you!" she screams.

I wanted to have the conversation, and she derailed me when she answered the door. I can't talk to her when she's like this. "I need to get home."

She drops her robe and says, "Just remember, there will be no more of this," as she displays her considerable breasts with brown areolas and large nipples, and her well-trimmed pussy.

"Goodbye, Celeste."

"Fuck you, you fucking drunk. Go to hell!" And she slams the door.

I broke up with her before going to college but continued to keep in touch with her. My mom is right. I should've probably cut off contact with her years ago.

THIRTY-SIX

EMERSON

*W*ORK CONTINUES to be crazy busy. I've managed to get my team at full strength, but we're still struggling with too much work and too little time.

Sara stops by my office. "It's after eight. It's just the two of us and Mason. Any interest in grabbing a drink downstairs with me?

I think about it for half a second. "I could use a nice bottle of merlot. I mean a glass," I say with a big smile.

"I could use a bottle myself, so I understand. Should we invite Mason?"

"Absolutely. The more, the merrier."

She goes off to find out if he's interested in joining us, and I pull up my Facebook page and search for Dillon. He hasn't made any recent posts. It's hard to stalk him if he isn't going to tell us what he's doing.

Sara sticks her head in my office once more. "He's going to join us. We're meeting in ten minutes by the elevators. Don't be late!"

WE WALK INTO THE BAR in the lobby of our building. It's packed full of people, but Mason sees an empty table in the corner and grabs it so we can have a bit of privacy but also watch what's going on.

The waitress approaches us. "Dinner menus?"

Sara says, "Yes, please."

She puts the menus down, and we look at them and order drinks: a glass of merlot for Sara and me, and bourbon for Mason.

Staring at the menus, Mason asks, "Have either of you spoken with Dillon? Or at least heard from him?"

We both shake our heads. "I'm collecting his mail and sending it to him at his mom's each week," I share. "I always write a short note to let him know how things are going and encourage him to call, but he never does."

"I've texted him a few times but haven't heard anything back. How about you?" Sara directs at Mason.

"I talked to him at his place about two months ago. I went over to tell him about our suspected mole, but he was drunk, his house was a wreck, and he was watching ESPN. He was still raw and angry. We exchanged words. Cameron and I talked about it, and we decided it was time to call in reinforcements. I called his mother to tell her how worried we were. Looks like she got him to come home."

The news makes my stomach roll. I want to call Dillon and beg him to come back.

"What will happen to us if he doesn't come back?" Sara asks.

"We'll worry about that if it comes, but I'm trying to be optimistic and wait. Pushing him to take a break was brilliant.

Thank you both for coming up with the idea," Mason says.

I suggest, "Let's talk about something different or I'll drink a whole bottle of merlot tonight. I promise you don't want to see me be that ugly." We all laugh. "Sara, how is your dating life going? It can't be any worse than mine."

"I hope yours is better than mine, because mine is going positively nowhere. What a mess it is to be single in this city," she bemoans.

Mason, whose eyes are a bit glazed over, says, "Sara, you have too much to offer. There's a good guy out there for you."

Sara blushes and gently elbows him in the side. "I'm not giving up yet. But if you know of anyone who isn't a client or competitor and is a reasonably nice guy—and single, of course— introduce us already." She turns to me. "And what about yours?"

Taking a big breath, I admit it isn't much better for me and I have no dating life. "I know. Terrible. I'm doomed to only be a dog mom forever. What about your love life Mason?"

He turns beet red and says, "I have someone I like, but I'm not sure she knows I exist. But you both know better than anyone the hours this job takes. I was thinking the other day how much I could use a sabbatical like Dillon."

"You know, six months is a long time, but what if the partners rotated through, each taking a month electronics-free. It's a good break. Maybe you can go climb Machu Picchu, Mason?" I suggest.

"I agree," Sara chimes in. "I mean why not? We work eighty to ninety hours a week, fifty-two weeks a year. It's well deserved."

Mason, apparently not sure about the idea, concedes, "The problem is there's never a good time. Let's look at some data once we know what's happening with Dillon." He's closed the discussion for now, but knowing he's interested in the possibility means it isn't closed forever.

We stick around until almost ten, talking about everything and touching on each of our suspicions as to who our mole is. None of us agree that it could be the same person, and then Sara says, "What if it's all of them?"

"I can't believe that's the case. We're a good employer, we do work with several companies, and there are some that aren't good." I look at my watch. "I need to get home. Poor Molly needs to get outside and have some quality time."

Mason pulls up his Lyft app and calls us three rides home.

Sitting in the back seat of the Acura MDX, I rest my head on the window. Watching the streets go by, I think about Dillon—his warm smile, bright blue eyes, and his blond curly hair. I miss him so much it hurts. I'm spending too much time thinking of him. I love the team at SHN, but I'm trying to be realistic with myself. If Dillon returns and we can't work together because of our history, I'll need to leave the company.

When I begin to cry, the driver asks if my boyfriend broke up with me.

"No, it's work related."

"You need a much less stressful job."

I can see him looking at me in the rearview mirror, and I meet his gaze, telling him, "You're probably right."

DILLON

I'M STILL NOT SLEEPING WELL, but I know my mom isn't sleeping well either. I can often hear her at night wandering the house, smell the coffee she makes, hear her cry. It's difficult to not be able to help her better with her grief. Lying in bed, the silence of the dark night moves my brain into overdrive.

I'm unable to quiet my mind, reliving conversations, occasionally with my dad or with Mason, Sara, Cameron, and Emerson. Mostly I think of better comebacks and retorts. Tonight, I'm primarily focused on the fight I had with Mason, all the things I should've said. But I know I should've said something simple like "I screwed up. I'm sorry."

I've been lying here for over three hours. My book doesn't interest me, but maybe if I watch some television, I can get my mind off the mess I've created and finally get some sleep.

Getting out of bed, I wander into the kitchen. I'm surprised to see my mom in her pink fuzzy bathrobe cinched at her waist, her eyes red and puffy from crying. "Hey, Mom." I put my arm around her shoulders and kiss her forehead.

"Hi, sweetie. Can't sleep either?"

"Nope. Work and how I need to fix it is weighing on my mind. And you?"

"Nights are the hardest when it comes to the loss of your father."

I reach for her and bring her in for a big bear hug. "It must get better eventually, right?"

She looks up at me with a forced smile. "That's what they tell me."

"What are you cooking?"

Shyly, she admits, "I warmed some milk, but it tastes awful."

"Sounds awful. Don't you have some chocolate we can add to it and make some hot chocolates?"

"Hot chocolate sounds much better."

I sit at the table as she grabs a bottle of chocolate sauce from the pantry and stirs it in. We sit in silence as the smell permeates the air as it warms on the stove top. I pick two random mugs and hand them to her. She pours the drinks, and we sit across from one another at the kitchen table.

I finally get up the nerve to tell my mom, "I feel like I let Dad down."

Putting her mug of hot chocolate down, she looks at me intently. "Why would you think that? I know he didn't feel that way at all."

"I wasn't here enough. I didn't call enough. I wasn't grateful enough for all Dad did for me."

"Is that why you're here? Because I don't think he expected anything like that. He loved you and your sister so much, and he was incredibly proud of you. You've accomplished so much.

Please don't ever think he was disappointed, because I know he wasn't.

"Thanks, Mom. I guess I needed to hear that." I reach across the table and grasp her hand. "I wish I could do more to ease your grief."

"You being here with me helps, I promise. I love you, Dillon, and I know your dad did, too."

EMERSON

As we jet down the 101 to Palo Alto in CeCe's red Mercedes convertible, I'm comforted by the thought that her parents have always been kind to me. I've known CeCe since we were assigned as roommates our freshmen year at Stanford. When we attended school, they insisted we come home every Sunday to do our laundry and have one decent home-cooked meal a week.

My folks are far away just outside Denver in Boulder, Colorado. They were actively involved parents when we were growing up, and are currently living a bohemian lifestyle refurbishing homes. My mom sits on the board of a non-profit which wants to save the prairie dogs and my dad teaches Environmental Studies at the University of Colorado. By all standards, I grew up upper middle class.

CeCe grew up as a member of the one percent. Her father was one of the original Silicon Valley billionaires, but as an Arnault, he grew up in a family that ran with the Rockefellers and Vanderbilts. You wouldn't know it though. They have a beautiful home and a full-time cook and housekeeper, but they're so down to earth. Her parents have such a healthy, loving, and respectful relationship, and are equally close with CeCe and her twin brother, Trey. Her parents' relationship is something CeCe and I both envy.

As we pull into the driveway, four dogs come running from the backyard and charge to meet us. CeCe gets down on the grass to greet them, and they attack her with licks and nudges for attention. I'm invisible, but mostly because they can smell the hotdogs she's brought them for a treat. They're hiding in a plastic bag in her purse and yet they can still smell them.

"You spoil those dogs," her dad can be heard saying, but I don't see him.

Looking up, I spot him in the tree picking apples. "Hey, Mr. Arnault."

"Three weeks in a row? Emerson, you're spoiling us."

The dogs, after eating their hotdog treats, come over to greet me and shower me with kisses, plus nudges for pats and attention. I should've brought Molly, but chaos would've ensued.

A male version of CeCe comes out of the house. "Mom, CeCe and Emerson are here. Hey, ugly," he directs at CeCe.

Before CeCe can respond, her dad says, "Okay Trey, that's enough. Leave your sister and Emerson alone."

CeCe turns to her brother and, in a motherly voice, retorts, "If I'm ugly, what does that make you?"

"Off to meet up with the guys. See ya!" He waves as he gets in his black Mercedes convertible.

We laugh and walk in to be greeted with hugs from CeCe's mom, the dogs following us.

"So wonderful to see you again this week, Emerson. We love

having you. I know we've said this for years, but please come even if CeCe wants to forget about us," she says as she hugs me.

"Mom! I don't want to forget about you. I want to cut some of the apron strings," CeCe exclaims.

Looking at her with admiration and love, her mom says, "Sunday night dinner is nice family time, with or without apron strings."

Standing with her hands on her hips, CeCe challenges, "I'm here, aren't I?"

CeCe bends to kiss her on the cheek. "Yes, dear. And I love you for it."

TREY DOESN'T MAKE IT BACK for dinner, but we have a good time anyway. Dinner conversation at the Arnaults' always reminds me of my family dinners: crazy, fun, and full of a lot of love and laughter. Since Trey was out and about, we managed some fun at his expense.

When the conversation turns to our dating lives, CeCe groans. "Daddy, you know men are scared of smart and accomplished women."

"Just don't give up," her mom tells us. "We all meet our soul mates at different times in our lives. You can't force it."

"We aren't giving up. We're just a little more career-focused right now," I explain.

CeCe's dad looks fondly at her mother and says, "You know it took me a while to get this woman to agree to marry me. I'm aware there is always hope."

CeCe rolls her eyes. "Mom was only reluctant because you were too busy to make time for her. As for me, there are only two other last names to have here in Silicon Valley—Jobs and Ellison—that make you a pariah. Guys either want to get to you"—she points to her father—"to invest in one of their adventures, or they're only interested in any money I might inherit."

"You know we want you to be careful, but we don't want you to build so many walls that they can't climb them," her mom says gently.

"Well, Mom, you know what they say: if we build an eight-foot wall, they'll make a ten-foot ladder," CeCe retorts.

"I think that's in reference to illegal immigration."

"It is, but it works here, too. Plus, I have my eye on someone, but he doesn't know it yet. I have to be stealth about my approach." CeCe confides.

Dripping with sarcasm, I ask, "What is stealth? Ignoring him? That's a surefire way to get his attention."

We're all laughing at this point.

As we leave for home, I'm the happiest I've been in many weeks. "Thank you for including me tonight. It was a lot of fun."

Looking at me with love, CeCe tells me, "Tonight was fun because you were there. I hope you know they expect you to come again next week."

"I got the hint from both your parents. I can't promise anything right now, but I'll try."

DILLON

*I*T'S SHORTLY AFTER EIGHT. I'm showered, the sun is shining, the birds are chirping, and I slept for five hours without interruption. I'm ready for a good day.

As I walk in the kitchen, I see my mom is dressed, reading the paper with a cup of steaming black coffee in her hand. "What's on the to-do list today?" I ask her.

"Well, it looks like there's a sale at English Gardens gardening center, so I thought we'd go over there and pick up a few things."

"If you're planning on planting where the juniper bushes were, we need to talk to the master gardener to find out what we need to do to the soil pH. Nothing will grow there otherwise."

She nods in agreement. "Leave in twenty minutes?"

"I'll be ready whenever you are."

WE SPEND THE MORNING at the garden center. Mom and the master gardener know each other by first names, and together they help to plan her gardens. She wants several annuals, and we'll do some soil replacement so we can plant some beautiful hydrangea and rhododendron flowering bushes, which will add color in the spring through summer.

"Wow, Mom, you went all out. This is probably a week's worth of work for the both of us."

"It'll be good for us. We need to keep our bodies busy so our minds can help us heal."

As I'm outside, working my hot afternoon away, I'm listening to a mix of Alternative music on my phone with my earbuds in. I'm in the front yard when suddenly there is a tap on my shoulder, and I jump what seems ten feet in the air.

I turn and look, trying to calm my racing heart. "Celeste! What are you doing here? You scared me."

"You left my house in such a panic last time we were together. You aren't returning my calls or texts. I want to talk."

"I think I said everything I need to say, Celeste." I run my hands through my hair out of nervousness. "I'm sorry if you feel I've led you on, but I don't care about you in *that* way."

She's wearing white short shorts and a red halter top with her nipples on high beams. When we were younger, that was all it took to get me going, and I know that's what she's trying to do now.

Shimmying up to me, she coos, "Oh, baby, I'll make you feel so good. We've known each other for so long. It would be a shame to throw it all away. I'm patient, and I won't tell her if you won't."

I take a deep breath. "Celeste, I know this is difficult for you to understand, but I don't have those kinds of feelings for you. I can only be your friend, nothing more. And I need you to leave me be and give me some space."

She pulls her halter top down, exposing her taut nipples, pulling and twisting them as she stares at me. In a raspy voice, she tells me, "You always make me wet."

I hear my mother say, "Celeste, I think Dillon asked you to leave. Please do as he asks."

Celeste turns ashen, and without looking at my mom or me, she spins around and murmurs, "Yes, ma'am."

We watch her go, and then my mom turns to me. "I think you've dodged a bullet with that one."

I smile down at her. "All because of you." And I kiss her on the forehead.

EMERSON

I'M MEETING with my team over a video conference. "Ladies, we were elected to organize the fall company picnic this year."

There's a lot of mumbling among the team, several not happy given how busy they already are. The picnic is truthfully a thankless job and too much work. I hear "How do we get ourselves unelected?" over the line.

Our newest team member, Wendy, says, "Obviously I've never been, but these parties are legendary in The Valley. What are they wanting, and what is our budget?"

I'm proud of my new employee for jumping in. "We've got a budget of two hundred and fifty thousand dollars. The partners would like it done in essentially four months, at the beginning of October, and they want it fun. Should we meet for lunch and brainstorm?"

Wendy asks, "What if I were to secure a party planner who would do it for free as long as she could use us as a reference?"

There is a lot of enthusiasm from the girls on the call, and I sigh in relief. "I would love the idea if we can get someone who's done these kinds of events before and can put it together quickly."

Wendy is a little hesitant, but finally shares, "My sister was doing the wedding of some Saudi princess, a five-million-dollar event with over a thousand people, but they decided to elope. It leaves her with a big hole in her calendar. I can ask her to put together some ideas and meet back with us next week, maybe over lunch down toward Palo Alto or Fremont?"

I can't believe our good fortune. "Wendy, are you sure she'd be interested?"

"She'd be thrilled. I'll confirm with her in case something came in for her this morning that I don't know about, but I know this is right up her alley."

"Great. We'll plan lunch for next Friday, and if your sister can do it, she can join us. If not, we're back to brainstorming. Moving on with our agenda..."

THIS IS THE FIRST TIME we're all meeting as a team face-to-face in some time. Wendy and her sister reserved a Vietnamese restaurant close to the university with a private room, and I'm the last to arrive.

Wendy walks up with a woman who could be her twin, dressed in a beautiful orange pastel floral print dress with long dark hair, big brown eyes, and flawless olive-colored skin. "Emerson, I'd like to introduce you to my sister, Tina."

Tina gives me a broad smile and extends her hand. "It's nice to meet you. Wendy has many great things to say about you. Thank you for giving me this opportunity."

"We're thrilled that you might be willing to take this on."

She smiles and says, "When you're ready, you can have a seat at the head of the table."

I thank her, and I greet each team member as I work my way to my assigned place. I make a point to ask each of them a personal detail. When I finally sit, I notice five easels covered and a projector set up. I'm stunned at how elaborate this may become.

Lunch is brought in by the staff of the restaurant, and we eat family-style while Tina presents her ideas. She's five feet tall in three-inch heels, but don't let that fool you—as soon as she opens her mouth, she's a true dynamo. So much energy, enthusiasm, and determination. I'd hate to be a vendor who crossed her.

"Thank you, ladies, for agreeing to meet with me. As you know, Wendy is my sister, so I've picked her brain on some options, and we've come up with ideas that I believe you're bound to like and share with the partners."

She spends the next hour going through the five ideas she has, each one better than the last. Her easels have drawings, locations, samples, and goodie bag ideas for each attendee. She has thought of everything—food, drinks, entertainment, and something for all ages. We're all hugely impressed.

We discuss and narrow it down to our favorite idea, and I'm prepared to pass it along to the partners. It's a fun afternoon, and not only do we get a lot of work accomplished, but we also get to have fun and eat well.

DILLON

CELESTE HAS CALLED so many times and texted nonstop that I put her home, cell, and work phone numbers on Do Not Disturb and block her. When the doorbell rings at 3:00 a.m., I'm concerned until I look through the peephole and see Celeste standing there. It angers me because I've told her I'm not interested, resorted to ignoring her, and yet she thinks her persistence will wear me down.

"What do you want, Celeste?" I growl as I answer the door.

Dressed in a see-through red baby doll negligee and curling her finger in her hair, she attempts to run another finger down my chest. "You, honey," she says seductively.

I push her finger aside, ignoring her provocative attire. "Celeste, I've told you many times that I don't feel *that* way about you. It's time you listen and leave my mother and me alone."

Not one to give up, she persists, "I can get beyond your cheating on me with *that* girl in San Francisco."

I've been clear. Now I'm angry. "Celeste. Go. Away."

Clearly determined, she steps forward and reaches for my

crotch. "You know how to make me feel good. I promise I'll make you feel good, too."

My mom speaks up from behind me, "Celeste, it's after three o'clock in the morning. Please go home."

Turning to my mom, Celeste says, "Mrs. Healy, your son proposed to me when we were fourteen years old. I gave myself to him. I've devoted my life to him. I've waited for him while he made money to support the future family we want to have."

Taking a deep breath, Mom puts her delicate hand on my back and stands close to me. "Celeste, I remember the day Dillon left for Stanford. I specifically remember he told you to move on, to find another boyfriend. You cried on the same front porch you're standing on right now. He broke up with you a long time ago. You need to go home. If you don't, I'll be forced to call the police."

Celeste, seemingly surprised by this, stands straight and becomes indignant. "Fine! Call the police. I bet they'd love to know how he's treated me," she screams as she backs away from the door and begins pulling at her hair. She's screaming over and over, something unidentifiable. I can't be sure exactly what she's saying, but I hear "No" repeated as she continues to pull at her hair and pace in the front yard, waving her arms.

She slips in the wet dirt and falls. Tears stain her face as she begins picking up wet dirt and throwing it at anything that catches her eye.

I don't realize my mom has stepped away until I hear her on the phone, talking to who I assume is the police, giving them our address. I'm stunned to see Celeste meltdown. It's like a train wreck you can't take your eyes off as you pass. Time moves slowly, yet the police seem to arrive quickly.

Various porch lights are coming on, and our neighbors are walking outside in bathrobes wanting to hear the commotion happening in our front yard. My mom and I are still standing at the door while Celeste is ranting and raving in our front yard, pulling up many of the new plants we planted earlier this week.

When the police officers arrive, they attempt to calm her with no luck. They call for the paramedics, who allow her tantrum to continue for several minutes while talking calmly to her. Celeste is covered from head to toe in mud, her face is tear-stained, her hair is a matted mess, and she keeps pacing. Eventually they soothe her and are able to get her in the ambulance and drive her away.

After the ambulance leaves, a policeman interviews both my mom and me. We explain what happened and her increasingly odd behavior. I share what happened after drinks at Harry's Bar, at her home when I went to join her for pizza, and her constant harassing phone calls. I'm embarrassed that my mother is hearing this, but it's essential they know.

The police officer finishes by asking if we'd like to charge her with trespassing and destruction of property. "I don't think so," my mom says.

He then adds, "She started with risky behavior and then moved to getting violent. If what you say is true and you both told her to move on, she then called so many times you blocked her call, and now she comes over in the middle of the night, I strongly suggest a temporary restraining order."

I quickly respond while looking at my mother, "I don't think we need to do that. Do you, Mom?"

"No, I think this will be enough of an embarrassment and,"

turning to me she adds, "You're leaving in a few days. Celeste won't be coming back."

"If you see her, either of you, call the police and reconsider the temporary restraining order," the officer tells us before he climbs in his car.

EMERSON

$\mathcal{A}$s I'm working out at the driving range, I get a message on my phone from one of our more high-profile clients.

TO: Emerson Winthrop
FROM: Tom Sutterland
SUBJECT: Need you to come in

Emerson,
Would it be possible for you and Mason to come by this morning? I need to speak with you both. It's important.

Tom

I quickly call Mason, who answers the phone out of breath. I can hear a treadmill running in the background. "Hey. I just got an email from Tom Sutterland. He would like the two of us to meet with him this morning, he says it's important. What does your calendar look like?"

"He doesn't say what he wants?"

"No, just that he would like us to come by this morning."

"I can only hope this has nothing to do with our mole. I'll clear my calendar. Can I pick you up at your place?"

My stomach tightens. I don't think this is going to be a fun meeting. I look at my watch and see it's almost six o'clock. "I'm at the driving range but can be home and ready in about an hour?"

"Great. See you then."

TO: Tom Sutterland
FROM: Emerson Winthrop
CC: Mason Sullivan
SUBJECT: RE: Need you to come in.

We'll be there as soon as traffic allows.

Emerson & Mason

Tom runs the up-and-coming social media company called PeopleMover. We're his sole investors and have provided him with three rounds of funding totaling better than one hundred million dollars and currently, we own over forty-three percent of the company. The word on Wall Street is they're going public and when they do, they'll go big, but they'll need one more round of funding before they can do so.

As we arrive, we're ushered from the lobby to his admin. An assistant leads us to an elevator that opens directly into his private office, a vast room occupying the corner of the building with floor-to-ceiling windows offering views of a vast courtyard.

The two remaining walls contained a door, a low bookshelf, and a single oil painting—a contemporary piece that reminds me of a Jackson Pollack. The black glass surface of his desk is equally uncluttered: a computer, a leather notebook, and a framed photograph of a nine-year-old boy.

We invested when he had an idea and a few friends helping him. Now he has over two thousand employees.

The admin explains he'll be with us in a few minutes and offers us coffee, soda, or water.

We wait less than five minutes when Tom comes in and sits across the desk from us. "Thank you both for coming on such short notice. What I'm going to tell you is not pretty." Sighing, he looks at us closely. "I met with Ben Klein yesterday of Perkins Klein. He presented me with this information."

My stomach hits the floor, flopping around like a fish out of water. I have no doubt the same is true for Mason.

He hands us a notebook, and with one look at it, we know it's our internal research about Tom and his company. In it, it shares how much we figure we can invest in his business for the final round, what we expect the stock to go public for inititially, and where we think it will land. Additionally, it has some research on each member of the management team, which, if taken out of context, could be brutal.

Taking a deep breath, Mason asks, "Did he tell you how he got it?"

"He told me with Dillon Healy out of the picture, things were imploding at SHN and people were sharing your information. He offered us more money for a smaller percentage of business so he can take us public."

The look on Mason's face confirms our worst fears. Someone we trust is sharing our internal research. I ask, "What did you tell him?"

"I told him I would think about it. But Mason, if he's getting confidential information from your employees and using it, I don't want to do business with him. This is extremely unethical to me."

"We appreciate your telling us, more than we can say. Are you looking for us to match Perkins Klein's offer?" Mason asks.

Folding his hands carefully in front of him, he takes a few moments to look at our eager faces. "Mason, you and Dillon gave me money when Perkins Klein wouldn't. I know things are unsettling with Dillon being out, but hopefully he'll return soon." He breathes deeply. "Let's stick with what you have in the proposal."

We're stunned. I didn't realize I was holding my breath until Tom gave us his answer.

Mason stands, extends his hand, and says, "We're proud to be a part of PeopleMover."

As soon as we're in the car, Mason calls Cameron and asks him to pull Sara into his office. With the four of us on the phone together, Mason shares what we found.

Cameron is the first to react. "Fuuuuuck. Thank God Tom is honest, but it also tells us who some of our friends are."

Sara says, "From a legal standpoint, if we figure out who's doing this, we can probably have them arrested and jailed for corporate espionage. But it'll be difficult to prove. Not that we aren't going to go after the mole vigorously, of course, but Perkins Klein is going to deny they paid for anything. They will insist the information came to them unsolicited and they didn't have anything to do with our downturn. They will also insist that they can't be sure where the information they passed along came from."

"We have a copy of the document," Mason says. "We need to put our finger on anyone who had access to the report and figure out how we're going to move forward."

"When I return to the office, my team and I will begin a search of all employee files, plus do another background check and a financial check on each employee. It'll cost us, but hopefully it can help us narrow down who might be vulnerable to espionage," I add.

We spend the remainder of our drive back to the office talking about our list of possible suspects. I finally ask, "Do we call Dillon and tell him? He's still officially a partner."

"I've been wondering the same thing. My gut says Dillon is on leave, so we should wait until he chooses to return. But I'll check with our law firm and verify," Mason tells me.

Looking out the passenger side window, I watch the rain fall and try to piece together what's happening.

DILLON

$\mathcal{A}$ S EACH DAY PASSES, my anxiety increases. I want desperately to be back at my firm. I miss having a purpose and a reason to get up every morning. I've enjoyed my break, but I think I'm starting to get restless.

In preparation for returning to work, I've been watching the trade newspapers and magazines, and I'm seeing Perkins Klein getting more and more business. It bothers me more than anything.

Over the years they've gone downhill. They've had a tough time securing new companies that seem to knock it out of the park. Until recently, they were investing in companies that were much further down the path of development and close to going public. Those are safe investments and because of that, they have smaller returns. It's what I always consider low-hanging fruit. These days they've been investing more in emerging concepts—which is our sweet spot. It isn't like them to chase young start-ups with angel and first-round funding.

As I'm reading the trades at the kitchen table on my tablet, newspapers spread across the table next to a notepad full of notes, my mom walks in. She pours herself a cup of coffee and looks at me. "You have a puzzled look on your face."

"I do?"

She sits with her elbows on the table, both hands holding her cup of coffee. As she peers over the top to take a sip, she says, "What's going on?"

With a heavy sigh, I sit back in my chair and stretch my long legs out. "I'm reading the trades and watching a competitor get business they typically wouldn't go after."

"I'm sorry."

Fighting to remain unemotional, I cross my arms over my chest. "I want to go back to my job. I want to fix this, and I want to fight for the company I've worked hard to build with my friends."

"You have two more weeks. Have you figured out what you want to say to them that will convince them to take you back?"

Without confidence, I explain, "I have numbers and figures ready to go."

She smiles. "Sweetheart, I don't think they doubt any of your 'numbers and figures,' but I think they may be looking for something else from you to take you back."

Leaning forward, closing my eyes, and holding the bridge of my nose, I whisper, "I'm sure they do. I don't know what to say other than sorry."

"Well, I think it's an excellent start, but you might want to take some time to apologize to each of the partners. Talk about what you did wrong and be sincere. But I only worked in the accounting department of a car manufacturing company. I never owned my own business."

I know she's right, but I don't know what to say to everyone that doesn't leave me begging and crying.

I have many restless nights thinking about what I did to the entire group. I behaved horribly toward each of them, and they deserve nothing less than heartfelt individual apologies, but I'm not sure I can be vulnerable. And what do I do if they still tell me it isn't enough for me to come back?

EMERSON

SITTING IN THE PARTNERS MEETING, I'm worried about Mason and Cameron. I can see the stress working them over. They've had six financial analysts go through the financial statements of four new prospective companies. We knew them inside and out. Most importantly, we limited those who had access to our information.

I evaluated these companies' owners, and if they had a team, I evaluated each of them as well. We have sound plans and we offer good money, yet we continue to lose them. The strain is becoming palatable. We've redone background checks, but nothing seems off or out of the ordinary with any of our employees.

"If we don't get Tsung Software, we may find ourselves looking at layoffs," Mason admits.

"What can I do?" Sara asks.

Cameron tells her, "I wish Dillon was here to sell this to Tsung. What were we thinking by asking him to take time off? What are we going to do if he doesn't want to come back?"

"We thought we were his friends. That we love him and he needed some time to heal," I say quietly.

With a noticeable sigh, Mason says, "You're right. We were being unselfish to send him on a break, but we must be strong. If he's going to come back drunk and belligerent, we can't take him back."

We all agree, but it still hurt to watch our earnings slip severely.

After our meeting ends, I wander by the employee lounge for my sixth cup of coffee this morning. A group of the marketing team is sitting around a table, becoming silent when I enter the room. I know they're worried; the Tsung Software is a possible big win for us.

I smile politely, greet them, and ask some general questions about the weather and upcoming weekend plans. Everyone is cordial, but no one is overly friendly. This makes my heart hurt. I take their disappointment personally.

EMERSON

I RECEIVE a text from Dillon: I'll be home late Wednesday. Would you like me to pick you up?

He doesn't respond to give me information on his return, so I have no way of tracking when he's arriving.

I'm anxious and excited to see Dillon. His distance over the last six months tells me he doesn't want a personal relationship with me, and I'm trying to be comfortable with that. But I miss my friend. I've not had anyone I could talk to about what is going on at SHN.

It takes me a half day of overthinking to realize that instead of letting a friend know he's coming, he's actually telling me that he doesn't need my help any longer. His lack of communication sends my brain racing into negative thoughts, putting a dark gray cloud over my head. I feel the loss of my friend like someone kicked me in the gut.

On my way home Tuesday night, I stop and pick up a few things for Dillon and for me from the grocery store. He may want the distance, but I'm determined to be civil. This way he isn't walking into an empty refrigerator.

I leave him milk for his coffee, bread, some fresh strawberries, and a dozen eggs. As I stop by his place for the final time, I leave behind his house key in a sealed envelope with his doorman, then cry over the sense of loss I feel once I leave his apartment. I miss him so much.

DILLON

I'VE BEEN IN DETROIT for almost five months. I have dinner most nights with my mom, I rarely drink, and I'm seldom going out with friends. We're in a comfortable routine, though I can't help but think I'm keeping her from things. I hear her friends offer rides to book clubs, bridge games, and afternoon tea, but she refuses. She tells them I'm visiting, but I can manage a night on my own and have told her as much. She just waves her hand like she's shooing a fly away and says, "Nonsense. I want to be with you."

We're talking about my departure over dinner, and Mom asks, "What are you going to do?"

Sounding more confident than I am, I state, "I want my company and Emerson back."

She gives me a broad smile with a lot of teeth. "Good. How are you going to do it?"

I lay out my plan, and she gives me some useful input.

As she drives me to the airport the next morning, I'm reflecting on the last few months being home in Michigan. "You know, Mom, I have no problem moving back and being with you for as long as you need me."

Almost swerving off the road, she says, "I don't want that from you, sweetheart." She grips the steering wheel tightly. "I want you to get your company back, and I want you to win Emerson back."

"Are you sure?"

"I'm positive. My friends miss me. It's time I got back to book club, my bridge group, and spending time with my friends. Plus, next time you return, I'm hoping Emerson is with you," she says with a mischievous grin.

"I love you, Mom."

"I love you, too." She hugs me tight at the security line, and I wave as I walk away.

I'll be back soon. I promise.

EMERSON

W E WALK THROUGH OUR AGENDA at the partners meeting. My second direct-report employee quit over fears she was going to get laid off, but we finally had a win on the board with Tsung Software, so at least there's some good news.

"Fiona's departure means we're down two people in my department. We're already tightly taxed right now, but I think this win is what we need so our employees will begin to feel safe about our viability," I share with the partners.

Mason says, "I know things are stressful right now, but we're still indeed viable, and we have plenty of money coming in the door. Are you looking for anyone?"

"We are," I assure him. "It's a tight market. I hate to lose good people over trade gossip."

"Me, too," Sara agrees.

"We've been working on the company picnic. Are you sure we want to do this grand a party?" I ask.

"Definitely. We want to show people we're healthy, stable, and growing," Mason states.

"Have we heard from Dillon?" Cameron questions. "The lawyer called me this morning and asked."

Mason says, "That's the next item on our agenda. I heard from Dillon yesterday, and he'd like to meet with us, though I'm not sure if I'm comfortable having him here at the office if he's going to blow up or be belligerent. I wanted to ask you all if you thought doing it at my place would work?"

We agree to meet on Monday afternoon at Mason's home with Dillon. My stomach turns at the thought of seeing him. I'm nervous yet excited. I hope he wants to come back. I miss him, and I'm hoping we can become friends again.

MASON'S HOME IS ON THE TOP OF NOB HILL, across from Huntington Park and Grace Cathedral. He lives in a beautiful high-rise, but in a garden apartment on the first floor behind the laundry room and parking garage. As you walk in, a dark, narrow hallway greets you, but it opens to a bright, giant living room and kitchen with a lot of natural light because it faces a colorful garden, with French doors leading to a backyard patio.

I'm surprised it's decorated with contemporary art on the walls. He has what I think is a Dale Chihuly glass art sculpture, the couches are a shade of light blue suede, and the side chairs are light green suede.

Mason has a beautiful golden Labrador retriever named Misty. She's a love, and greets us all with plenty of licks and nudges before leading us out to the stunning patio, with views of the neighboring buildings covered in ivy and a giant fig tree shading the backyard. There are flowers and even a spot of green lawn, an oasis within the walls of apartment building.

Mason has beers for us to drink and we chat, all of us nervous waiting for Dillon's arrival.

DILLON

THIS IS THE MOST DIFFICULT meeting of my life. I walk around Huntington Park for twenty minutes, taking in the mothers pushing strollers and the view of Alcatraz on a beautiful cloudless day before heading to Mason's. I don't know what I'm going to do if they turn me down.

I finally get up the nerve to ring the bell, and of course Misty greets me. I love this dog almost as much as I love Emerson's Molly.

As I follow Misty, butterflies in my stomach, I see everyone is on the back patio.

Cameron walks up, shakes my hand, and gives me a "manly" hug—the kind that's less an embrace and more back slapping.

Mason is behind him and does the same, saying, "Good to see you, man."

Sara gives me a big hug. "We've missed you."

Emerson is standing back. She was kind to me while I was gone, despite the fact that I was such an ass before I left. I was the worst to her and owe her the biggest apology.

I walk in to give her a warm embrace and whisper in her ear, "Thanks for all you did while I was gone, and for leaving me some staples. They've been much appreciated." She smiles, and it warms my heart.

Mason asks, "So, how was your time away?"

"It was well needed. Thank you all for making me do something I didn't know I wanted or needed. I went home to my mom's and helped her out with a few things around her house. There was no alcohol and"—I look directly at Emerson—"no girls."

They all take a seat and I remain standing. I have notes, but as I begin to talk, I abandon them and speak from my heart.

"I owe you all so much. Mason and Cameron, we met our first day in the dorms at Stanford. We were young and naïve, but we formed an instant friendship which has lasted through school, grad school, women, jobs, and together we founded SHN.

"Mason, you've been the leader of our group. You pulled each of us in when we attempted to go astray. You've led us from being a gangly group of three guys with too much money to being responsible for almost seventy-five employees, and taking over one hundred companies from angel funding to sale or taking them public. Without your leadership, Cameron and I would probably be in our first apartment in La-Z-Boy recliners watching *Sports Center*. As our leader, you also helped to realize I was struggling. Having lost your own father just before we met, you knew the signs. Calling my mom was a low blow, but having been there, you knew we both needed each other. I'm sorry I wasn't a good partner, and more importantly a better friend."

Mason nods at me as a clear acceptance of my apology.

"Cameron, you're the heart and soul of our company. Your brain functions at warp speed. You look at technology like no one I've ever seen. Without your knowledge and understanding, we would never have invested in companies such as Silly Sally initially. We definitely wouldn't be here today, enjoying what we both call legalized high-stakes gambling. I know when everything with me went south, you had to make a tough call, and I know you well enough to know you laid awake for hours agonizing over your decision to approach the group. I'm sorry I put you in that position."

Cameron also nods at me.

"Sara, without you, we would be three guys without a dime to our names. We would've spent and given all our money away. We don't appreciate you enough for all you do for us, me most of all. Despite my taking you for granted, dumping things on your desk late on Friday afternoons or being ignorant of you and your feelings, I know you're the heartbeat of our company. Without a heart, we wouldn't be here today. I'm sorry for being such an ass to you. I promise that, if given a chance, I'll do better."

She wipes a tear from her eyes and nods her acceptance.

"Emerson, this is the hardest apology of all. I treated you poorly. Professionally, my behavior was inappropriate. There is never an excuse to yell at anyone ever. Your analysis is always spot-on, and it was wrong of me to ever question it. For that I'm sorry. I also owe you many apologies on a personal level, which I'm hoping you will allow me to make in a more private setting, but I want to be sure you know how sorry I am for being a jack-ass and taking advantage of our friendship. I'm genuinely sorry, and I hope you'll allow me the opportunity to make it up to you."

Emerson gives me a slight smile, and I'm not sure she's accepting my apology.

This is hard for me, but I continue. "Sara and Emerson, I know this leave of absence would never have happened without you both. I know both these guys love me as a brother but didn't know how to manage my crazy behavior, so thank you both for thinking of a possible solution that allowed me the chance to lick my wounds and get my head on straight. If you're kind enough to take me back, I promise to not ever repeat what happened.

"I want my job back. I miss all of you, and I miss our company and the difference we're making in The Valley. I want to be clear, I desperately want to come back, but I want to be honest with all of you." Looking directly at Emerson, I say, "I can't return if I can't have a relationship with Emerson. She's the light of my world, and while I owe her more apologies than I'll ever be able to say, she's the person I want and the person I need. I know we talked about giving too much power if we were to couple up, but I can't come back if we have to hide our relationship. Emerson, you mean too much to me to pretend we aren't together. I want to shout from the rooftops how I feel about you."

Speaking to the group, I continue. "I know my request to explore a relationship is a lot to consider, but be assured that if you take me back, I commit one hundred percent to being sober, kind, and a strong partner you can depend on. Please allow me to come back."

Everyone is sitting in stunned silence.

Eventually, Mason stands. "Dillon, we all appreciate where you are. If you could give us the chance to discuss your terms, I can text you when we have an answer."

FORTY-NINE

EMERSON

*T*HE DISCUSSION IS HEATED, Cameron fuming. "No fucking way can he make these demands." He turns to me. "How long have the two of you been together?"

I stammer, "We were never 'together.'" They all look at me, clearly expecting more. I try to deflect, but it isn't enough, so I break down and tell them about Adam, how I was working myself to death because every time I tried to sleep, I would relive that night. I share that Dillon stayed with me every night so I could sleep, and how he helped to nurse me back to life, but I stress that it was never sexual. I then share with them his devastation over his father's death, and again we were back to spending every waking minute together until he went off the rails. I did gloss over the short time that we were more than friends.

"Dillon's request is completely a shock to me. I'm not sure if I want a relationship with him," I state.

We talk for over three hours. I know they want Dillon back; he brings a piece we're missing. Finally, I say what everyone is thinking. "We need Dillon back. I'm less pivotal to the organization. Maybe what we need to do is figure out how to transition me out. He's much more important to this company than I am. You can buy me out, and I'll leave. I'll commit to not competing in the same industry or start another competing business."

Cameron puts his hand on my knee. "You're equally important, and you're being willing to give it up so we can have Dillon back tells me you need to stay."

Sara begins to cry. "I can't believe you're willing to walk away from all this for Dillon. That is true love."

I chuckle nervously. "Slow down, Sara. I'm not sure I want a relationship with Dillon after everything that's happened."

Mason, who has been sitting back and listening this whole time, finally says, "We're growing, and we'll be adding more partners in the years to come. We're no longer a group of four. Emerson, we want you to stay, and we want Dillon to return. I reserve the right to ask one or both of you to leave if it becomes a problem, but I think we can make this work."

I nod my agreement.

Mason texts Dillon. Please come back. We've made a decision.

DILLON

*A*FTER WALKING AROUND the park the first hour, I've been sitting across the street in the bus shelter. I thought thirty minutes was a long time, but three hours has me worried. My demand may have backfired, but I need Emerson, and I want to have an actual relationship with her. The text notification makes me nervous.

I walk in and Mason embraces me. "Welcome back."

"Took you guys long enough. I was sweating it."

"We admit it, our hang-up was your special request to be more open with Emerson," Cameron explains.

"I figured that was the problem. I spent the last six months watching the trades and thinking about all the shit I did wrong. I also thought a lot about Emerson, and I realized I screwed up and wanted her in my life."

"Well, she must really like you," Sara shares. "She threw herself in front of the bus and offered to leave the company so you could return."

I turn to Emerson. "You did?"

She nods. I knew I loved her before, but that seals the deal. "A lot has happened since you left. We need you," she says softly.

Then Sara tells me the bad news. "We have a mole at the company, and we can't figure out who's feeding our internal documents and research to Perkins Klein."

I can't believe what I'm hearing. How is it possible that we have a corporate spy? "Are you kidding?"

Mason, pinching the bridge of his nose, takes a deep breath and says, "I wish we were."

"Jeez. What are our next steps?"

We spend what's left of the afternoon talking and strategizing, and we eventually order dinner. I also share with the partners four companies I think we should chase for angel, first round, and even the second round of funding.

I pull out four proposals with my own research, and we pour through them until after midnight. We all agree to meet again at the office tomorrow morning. Each of us needs to do our due diligence to make sure the investments are viable on all fronts.

Cameron says, "I have an idea. As long as our due diligence works out, what would you all think if only the four of us pitch Dillon's suggestions? Only the four of us are involved. We then pick four duds. Four companies that look good but may not have the right technology or a good team to pull it off, and we have our teams chase them. We know we won't bid the money, but we'll trust our mole to share. Perkins Klein can fund the duds, and we'll be home free to bid these four without worry about the mole sharing."

We all agree it's a good idea and work through the details. It's nice having the team together again.

As we're leaving, I ask Emerson, "Would you be willing to share a Lyft?"

I can see the conflict in her eyes, but she nods.

As we get into the car, she turns to me. "I'm not spending the night with you. We will drop you off, and we will talk. Eventually."

"Look, Emerson. I know this was a surprise, and I should've talked to you about it before I did it, but I wanted to make sure you knew you were important to me and I don't want to be at SHN without you. I've been in love with you since the first day we met. I need you, Em. Please take me back. I need your sweetness to balance out the asshole in me. I need your generous heart to remind me that not everyone cares about money. I need to be wanted for something other than my bank account. I need you to fight with me when I'm giving you too much shit."

She doesn't look at me, just sighs. "Dillon, I'm upset with you. Not only did I need to essentially tell them I would leave everything I worked for so they could have you back, but I had to explain everything that happened with Adam. I'm a private person. I'm not happy that you put me in this situation."

I'm surprised to hear how difficult the conversation was because of my simple demand. "I'm sorry. That was not my intention. I know we can't pick up where we left off, but I thought maybe tomorrow night I could come over after work and we go for a run with Molly, maybe have dinner at that café we both like by your house."

"I suppose."

"Can I pick you up in the morning and drive you to work?"

"What time?" she asks hesitantly.

"Seven?" I lean over and give her a hug goodbye. She smells good, just like I remember. It feels so right to have her in my arms.

"I'll be ready."

EMERSON

*D*RIVING BACK to my house, I'm having trouble digesting all that's happened today. I have feelings for Dillon, but he made me tell all the partners about a dark time for me. He also hurt me and shut me out these past six months.

Despite the late hour, I call CeCe when I get home and tell her about my day.

"He told the partners he wanted an open relationship with you or he didn't want to come back?" she asks.

"I'm more shocked than you are. It came out of left field for me, too."

"You haven't mentioned him in a long time. How do you feel about his act of love?"

"I thought about him every day, but I was devastated by how he treated me before he left, cutting off all communication. I sent him a note every week when I forwarded his mail, and never once did he reach out to me. I guess, to be honest, I'm hurt."

"I don't blame you, sweetie, but he's risked a lot to require your relationship be in the open. It might be worth at least a conversation or two to figure out what he's looking for. Make sure you protect your heart though. You're beautiful on the inside and the outside. Don't let him crush you again."

"I promise."

"Remember, if he tells you he wants a fuck buddy, tell him you aren't a sex toy and to fuck off."

I giggle at that. "Have a good night. I may not see you until Sunday, but I'll be joining you at your folks'."

DILLON ARRIVES WITH COFFEE IN HAND a few minutes before seven. He leaves his running clothes behind and gives Molly some love.

As we drive in, he tells me, "I know I screwed up by not running my idea past you last night. I didn't want you to tell me it was a bad idea. I'm sorry. But my thought is during work hours, we only discuss work. We don't flirt or sext, and I'll try my hardest to not want to bend you over my desk and fuck you ten ways to Sunday."

I laugh at his remark. "I think that'll work for now. But I also believe we're going to need a few more rules, so the rest of the partners don't feel like we're a voting bloc."

"Agreed." We're quiet a few moments, and then he adds, "I owe you a better apology, and if you give me a chance, I'll begin tonight and again every night. I was a jackass. I was hurting and took it out on you—the one person who was kind to me. I promise to do everything I can to make it up to you."

He parks in his reserved spot, and I lean over and kiss him on the cheek. We'll figure this out. He holds my hand until the elevator opens on our floor. We haven't walked five feet into the office before Dillon is bombarded with the employees all welcoming him back.

I leave him to catch up with everyone and walk into my own office. In my email, I find Sara has put me on Dillon's calendar to go over his proposals with him and contribute any thoughts.

Mason orders a special lunch to celebrate Dillon's return, and it's a huge celebration.

Mason taps a spoon on the counter to get everyone's attention. "I want to formally welcome Dillon back to SHN."

There is polite clapping and a lot of "Hear! Hear!"

"Dillon, this place is not the same without you. For those of you who haven't heard, we've identified four companies to chase, and everyone will have a role in getting us up and ready to pitch to them. We've got a lot of work in front of us, but I know we can do it."

There is more clapping, and the overall morale of the company seems to have more than doubled. Employees are excited again, and for the first time in weeks, I believe we're going to be okay.

DILLON

THE FIRST DAY BACK is exhausting. It's almost seven, and we've had nonstop work all day. I instant message Emerson: Ready to head out in 15 minutes?

Works for me. I'll meet you at the elevator.

ANNABEL seems to be waiting for me on my way to the elevator. She walks up and asks, "You up for getting a drink tonight?"

As Emerson approaches, I tell her, "I'm going running with Emerson tonight."

"Have fun. Oh, I think I forgot my cell phone. See you both in the morning." And Annabel runs off, leaving us to ride down in the elevator alone.

I grab Emerson's hand again, and she gives it a gentle squeeze.

When we get into the car, she leans over and kisses me on the cheek. My heart races and my stomach flips.

"I haven't completely forgiven you, but I did miss you, and while I haven't actually said it, I want you to know how glad I am that you're back." She smiles at me, and my heart melts.

"I want you to know I'll spend the rest of my life making it up to you."

"Well, right now I need a run to get this stress worked out so I can sleep tonight."

"I know another way you can work that stress out." I wink and smile at her.

She laughs, pushes my arm, and says, "You wish."

And she's right. But I know I'll have to take it slow to get her back in my bed again.

As we run toward the Golden Gate Bridge, we talk about how things went in Michigan. I tell her everything, even what happened with Celeste.

I'm so out of shape that I barely make it and insist on stopping at the same Italian restaurant we had dinner that first night.

"This place has good memories," I tell her.

She doesn't look at me as she glances over the menu. "It does?"

"Yes. This is the first meal we shared outside of work."

Looking up from the menu, she replies, "You're right. It was a good night. The first of many good nights together."

Her honesty warms my heart and leaves me hope for a future together. "I did miss you while I was gone."

"I missed you, too. But I'm not sure what I want from you. Dillon, you hurt me the last time we were together."

It's hard to hear that I hurt her, but I know I did, and I deserve for her to tell me all about it. "I know. And I hurt you intentionally. My life was a mess, and I was scared of how I felt about you. But that's not an excuse, and I'm sorry. And I'm not kidding, if you give me a chance, I'll make it up to you every day for the rest of my life."

"Let's take it one day at a time."

The sun is setting behind her, giving her the aura of an angel's halo. I don't think I've ever loved her more than right now. She's given me hope for a future, of a life we might be together. One day at a time is a start.

After a comfortable dinner, we walk back to her house. I'm pretty sure she doesn't want me to come in, so I ask, "May we do this again tomorrow? And for the rest of the week? I need the exercise, and I want to spend time with you. And maybe I can set up a tee time for Saturday?"

"You sure are persistent," she says, smiling. "I'll commit to running tomorrow and to Saturday. Let's play the other days by ear. I work for this crazy company that doesn't give me much of a personal life."

I laugh at her joke. "Well, let me know when you want me to talk to someone. I'll go in and give them a real talkin' to and get you more personal time." She giggles, and I love the sound. "I'll pick you up in the morning?"

"I'll be ready. Good night, Dillon."

"Good night, Emerson."

EMERSON

*W*E'VE MET and run every night for the last four nights, and have hit all three restaurants in the neighborhood. "I can't take eating another meal in my neighborhood. I thought we could order in from the Greek restaurant in your neighborhood and have them deliver to my place. It's dinner and nothing more, of course."

"I'll do whatever you want."

I stop and turn to him. "While it's nice to get my way, our relationship should be give and take." I touch his arm. "I want to do what you want to do, too."

"Well then, since the restaurant is in my neighborhood, why don't we eat at my place?"

"Okay then, since you'll feed most of the pita bread to Molly, I want an extra order of pita bread."

During a lovely dinner sitting at his dining room table, he asks, "How about Saturday night we have a real date?"

"Other than playing golf?"

"Yes. We dress nice, and I pick you up at your house. We head to a nice quiet restaurant where they wait on us. We drink a little wine and enjoy lots of conversation, maybe take a walk after dinner and hold hands. And maybe, just maybe you'll let me kiss you good night on your doorstep when I drive you home."

"I think I'd like that."

WHEN I get home, I text CeCe:

> Emerson Winthrop: I have a date with Dillon on Saturday night. A real date!
>
> CeCe Arnault: Finally! What are you going to wear?
>
> Emerson Winthrop: Something black.
>
> CeCe Arnault: What about that dark blue backless lace dress?
>
> Emerson Winthrop: That may be a message I'm not ready to send.
>
> CeCe Arnault: So you'd rather wait for a guy who's emotionally unavailable, insecure, and lives with his mother?
>
> Emerson Winthrop: No. I already found those guys and gave them back, but thanks for the gentle reminder of all the great guys here. I'll wear the blue dress and my pair of Louboutin sandals.
>
> CeCe Arnault: I'll give you my 1 p.m. appointment with Marco for a blowout. We need to get you a pedicure and bikini wax.
>
> Emerson Winthrop: I'll leave it in your capable hands. I need to get some sleep. I have a golf date with Dillon, and he's picking me up at 6:30.

CeCe Arnault: In the morning?

Emerson Winthrop: Yes. Good night.

CeCe Arnault: Good night. Call me tomorrow after your golf game.

Dillon drives up in his SUV and I kiss Molly goodbye as I run out the door, golf clubs in hand. "You're early."

"I didn't know how long it was going to take to get coffee." He walks around the car and looks at me, stopping in his tracks. "You look fantastic."

I'm wearing a white golf skirt with a blue geometric pattern and a dark blue T-shirt. Blushing a brilliant shade of pink, I say. "Thanks. I've worn this before."

"Oh, I remember. Trust me, I do remember." Dillon smiles wide as he looks me up and down. I roll my eyes and smile, and we set off, driving in silence as we enjoy the beautiful Northern California sunrise and our hot coffees.

I'm deep in thought when Dillon asks, "We still on for tonight?"

"Yes, of course. I have to meet up with CeCe this afternoon, but I should be ready. What time do you plan on picking me up?"

"Well, we have dinner reservations at eight. How about I pick you up at seven, and we can enjoy a drink beforehand?"

"Sounds good. Are you telling me where we're going?"

He gives me a big smile. "You'll see. I think you'll like it."

I'm not sure what his plan is, but I believe it'll be a fun night.

We drive up to the club with enough time to hit a few warm-up balls on the driving range.

We're paired with two men Dillon knows but I've never met. As we drive up to the first hole, I see the guys are playing from the middle tees. I start to tell them I play from the back, but Dillon puts his hand on my arm and discretely shakes his head.

After the three men play, Dillon tells them, "Watch this."

They're speechless when I walk to the back tees and tee off, driving within a few yards of them.

Dillon seems proud as a peacock and says, "Boys, I'd like you to meet my girlfriend, Emerson Winthrop. She played for Stanford and had an invite to play in the LPGA. I hope you're ready to get your asses handed to you."

My game is a little off this round, having been too busy to get out and practice, but I still enjoy the morning with Dillon. As we finish the final hole, I lose only to him—which in itself is a first. I killed the other guys by over a dozen strokes, but they were good sports about it. They're kind and invite me to play with them anytime.

Dillon is almost giddy. "I've never beaten you at golf. That was awesome!"

"You do know that if you do what you proposed to the partners, it's bound to happen a lot, don't you?"

"Maybe. I know you haven't been able to practice much, but you're still a single digit handicap and we're playing from the back tees. Truly you killed me, but I'll revel in the win until I get you home."

On our drive back into The City, he asks, "You didn't let me win did you?"

"Never. I'm way too competitive, and I know your ego isn't wounded if you lose. You won fair and square."

"Can I tell Mason and Cameron?"

"As long as you also tell Sara."

He drives up to my house to drop me. "Good point. I'm texting everyone now."

I laugh. "There goes my afternoon."

Turning to face me, he reaches for a stray curl that's escaped and pushes it behind my ear. "I can't wait for tonight. See you at seven."

He leans in, and I give him a slow, lingering kiss. "I'm looking forward to it."

Getting out of the car, he pops the trunk and pulls my clubs out, then kisses me once more. We wave goodbye, and I head inside.

I HAVE LESS THAN AN HOUR to get showered and over to CeCe's hairdresser. When I arrive at the salon in black yoga pants and a white button-up shirt, CeCe meets me with two glasses of champagne. "One for you and one for me."

Taking the glass, I tell her, "Thank you. Is Andre ready for me?"

"Not quite yet. He'll take you after we get you a bikini wax and a pedicure."

"Bikini wax? I'm not sure I'm ready for Dillon to be close enough to see my bikini line."

Putting her arms around me, she holds me close and says, "Honey, you've been pining away for Dillon for the last six months. You don't have to do anything you aren't comfortable with, but if it happens, it's important to be prepared."

"Fine," I say, shaking my head.

What did I get myself into?

Two hours later, I'm hairless, painted, and blown out.

"You look mah-vo-las, dahling." CeCe coos.

I give her a big hug and a kiss on the cheek. "Thank you. I still don't know where we're going, but I think I'm ready for just about anything."

With a twinkle in her eye, she squeezes my arm and says, "Enjoy yourself. He's working hard to win you back. I'm sure it isn't a play. Call me when you get home tonight... or maybe tomorrow morning," she singsongs.

DILLON

I'M NERVOUS to pick her up. I spent the afternoon shower-ing and making sure I'm well groomed. Tonight needs to go well. I've never needed anyone, but I need her in my life. I love her, and I want to make sure she knows that. I understand that she may not be ready to be intimate with me, but I'll wait for her as long as it takes.

When I arrive at her door, I have a bouquet of red roses and a treat for Molly. Taking a big breath, I brace myself before ring-ing her doorbell. *Please let tonight go well.*

When she opens the door, she takes my breath away. "Wow! You look positively beautiful."

She blushes a deep shade of pink and gives me a big smile. "Thank you. So do you." Turning to hold Molly back, who can smell I have a treat for her and is going crazy for it, I see Emer-son looks as good going as she does coming. Her dress is conser-vative from the front but sexy as hell from the back, a subtle hint of a chain at the nape of her neck with a bare back. Makes me want to slip my hand into her dress. It's going to take all of my restraint to not want to throw her down and make passionate love to her every five minutes.

"Molly, down!" she says.

"It's my fault. I stopped at the butcher and picked up a good beef bone for her to enjoy while you're out tonight." Taking it out of the package, I give it to Molly, who immediately runs off with it to her crate.

Laughing, Emerson locks Molly in the crate and turns to me. "She already loves you. Now she's going to want to move in with you."

"Only if her mother wants to come with her," I say with an endearing smile as I hand her the roses.

"Thank you." She steps up and gives me a demure kiss on my cheek before taking the flowers. I follow her to the kitchen as she pulls a vase out of a cabinet and fills it with water. "These are stunning and so thoughtful."

"Tonight is very special." I take her by the hand and lead her out to the Town Car. The driver runs out to open the doors for us.

"Are you going to tell me where we're going?"

"I suppose I can. I've reserved a table at Boulevard Restaurant that's facing the water, with views of Treasure Island and the East Bay."

She smiles at me. "Very romantic." Her hand rests on my knee, and she leans in. Her closeness sends jolts of energy to my groin, and I'm desperate to show her what she does to me.

My stomach tightens as I let my eyes run down the long line of her legs. Her dress is pretty, sensual, yet not over the top. I rein in my desire to ravage her and we head to dinner.

As we walk in the restaurant, I hold her at the waist and kiss her on the forehead. We let the hostess know we've arrived and will be at the bar having a pre-dinner drink.

Sitting down, Emerson asks, "Are you okay to drink? I don't mind drinking tea or soda if you've given up alcohol."

My heart melts even further as she thinks of me and my needs. "I think I'll be fine. I haven't given up liquor—yet."

I signal the bartender, and he walks over. "Welcome, Mr. Healy."

"Hi, James. Can we have a bottle of the 2009 Cristal?"

"Of course, sir. Would you prefer a quiet table here at the bar until your reservation? I can bring you the bottle in a side ice bucket."

"That would be perfect. Thank you."

As we sit at the small side table and get comfortable, I look at her through the candlelight. I'm not sure she could be more beautiful than she is sitting across from me with the sun setting behind her. My heart is racing in my chest, so much so a light sheen of sweat covers my hands and forehead. It's almost embarrassing.

The bartender sets up our champagne and pours us our glasses. Raising the glass, I look into Emerson's eyes. "Thank you, Emerson, for everything you did for me after my dad's passing. And thank you for giving me a second chance I don't deserve."

We toast to our future, and we drink and talk. The conversation runs from our friends to work. and we wind up discussing the corporate espionage until we move to our dinner table.

It's comfortable to be here with her. I don't feel the need to impress her. She's seen the worst in me and is still sitting across from me.

As I look at her, I know without a doubt that I love her.

EMERSON

DINNER IS INCREDIBLE. Dillon ordered for us in advance, and we start with raw oysters, followed by an arugula salad and scallops in a butternut squash puree. Each course comes with a glass of a different California wine.

As dessert arrives, I tell him, "I'm not sure I can eat another bite."

"But it's your favorite, key lime pie."

"I'm going to burst out of this dress."

"I wouldn't mind seeing that," he says with a huge grin.

As we eat our dessert, Dillon seems to be struggling to tell me something. It takes time, but he finally fesses up. "I know I screwed up, but I want you to know that I did this not because of what a jerk I was, but because Adam was a jerk."

I just look at him, not sure what he's going to say. At the mention of Adam's name, I want to bolt from the table, but he reaches for my hand and rubs his thumb lightly across my skin.

"CeCe and I sat down and talked before my dad died. We put a plan in motion. When I confronted Adam, he mentioned that he had your escapade recorded on video."

My hand goes to my mouth, my breathing shallow and fast. "Oh no!" I'm beginning to feel dizzy, but he reaches for my hand again and gives it a comforting squeeze.

"In our business, we know a few people who are black hats. Do you know what a black hat is?"

I nod. "Yes, it's a hacker who does illegal things."

"Exactly. Well, CeCe and I devised a plan. We used one of my black hat contacts, and we broke into Adam's cloud accounts and erased his storage. We then had two people go into his house, fill the bathtub with water, and dump his laptop and tablet. At the same time, he was pickpocketed, and his cell phone was stolen."

"Are you kidding?"

"No. We wanted to be sure Adam didn't have any copies of the video that he could recall and download on another device. That's where CeCe suggested we stop. I know it would've been enough, but I'm still angry about what he did to you, and I believe several other women. We were sure if we got the police involved, it would've been ugly and hard on all of you. You didn't need to be victimized again."

"Oh God!" I moan.

"However, without CeCe's knowledge, I may have directed the black hats to do some naughty work. We might have gotten access to his credit history and blew up his credit. Oh, and deleted the last four payments on his mortgage. And maybe maxed out all his credit cards."

I sit back in my chair, laughing at his antics. "You didn't! I can't believe you did that for me."

"Emerson, you've always been the woman for me. I knew the

minute I saw you speak at the Venture Capital Silicon Valley conference."

It all hits me then, and tears run down my face. A video would've ruined me, and he protected me. I agree that I couldn't have been Adam's first. He was too good. Many women will thankfully never know, and my friends have hopefully prevented Adam from further ruining their lives. And if he's smart, he won't do it again.

Reaching across the table, I cup his cheek. "You're amazing. Thank you." I lean over and kiss him softly.

Dillon pays our bill, and we walk the waterfront hand in hand. It's such a beautiful night as the fog rolls in, but it soon becomes chilly. I shiver, and Dillon immediately removes his suit coat and puts it over my shoulders. As I warm from the heat it carries, I tell him, "Now you're going to be cold."

He looks down at me and smiles. "I don't mind. I want to take care of you."

I search his eyes to see if he's telling me what he thinks I want to hear, but I can't be sure. I'm trying to protect my heart. If he were to break it again, I don't think I could ever recover.

He puts his arm around me, holding me close, and I squeeze him tight.

We stop at the waterfront, and I can feel the heat emanating from him. "Incredible," I tell him as we watch the traffic drive over the Bay Bridge and the moonlight play across the bay.

Calling the driver of our car, Dillon lets him know we're ready to leave. "Let's get you home," he says as he leans down and kisses me deeply. I allow his tongue entrance into my mouth, and the kiss sends pulses to my core. I lean in and feel his erection at the apex of my thighs. He wants me, but I don't know what I want yet.

Breaking the kiss as the car arrives, he opens the door for me before the driver is able to.

During the drive, we hold hands and I rest my head on his shoulder. Before I know it, we're pulling in front of my house. He asks the driver to wait for him as he will be right back.

Walking to my front door, I have mixed feelings about his leaving quickly. He leans down and gives me a passionate kiss. "When you're ready and not before then. See you tomorrow?"

Nodding, I whisper, "Yes. See you tomorrow." Standing on my tiptoes, I put my arms around his neck, smelling his cologne, and kiss him aggressively. My core is pulsing, and I know my panties are wet.

Pulling away, I turn and walk into the house, waving good-bye as he gets in the car and leaves.

EMERSON

M Y BRAIN is telling me to not get involved, but my body wants and needs him. I think of him all night, replaying the romantic evening in my head over and over, dissecting it. Dillon was a perfect gentleman all night. I think I'm still stunned that he would protect me by essentially destroying Adam. I'm shocked at how it makes me feel better. I didn't know any videos existed, but I guess my subconscious knew and was worried. Knowing the video no longer exists has lifted an enormous weight off my shoulders.

We talked about meeting tomorrow, but I have no idea what his plans are. I can't get my brain to quiet and stop going through my mental to-do list.

I need to get work done on the secret companies we're approaching.

I'll need to get some of my anxiousness and stress taken care of through a good run.

I want to spend some good quality outside time with Molly. Maybe a run can do that.

My house could use a good scrub. It's neat and clean, but a

bit dusty.

I'm getting tired of ordering in lunch every day at work. I know the break room has lunch, but it isn't calorie friendly. I'm starting to skip the meal, which isn't good for my afternoon energy. Maybe there's something I can make so I can pack each day for work. And it can't be a salad.

I need to see Dillon. I want him to hold me. I want him to tell me everything is going to be okay.

I FINALLY FALL ASLEEP and wake to hear someone knocking at my door. I'm startled by it, and Molly is barking like crazy. It's after nine according to the clock. I never sleep this late. How did that happen?

Pulling on a pair of yoga pants, I peek through the peephole and see Dillon.

"Good morning," he greets when I open the door. Looking me up and down, he asks, "I'm sorry. Were you sleeping? I can come back later."

"No! I mean yes, I was sleeping, but I don't ever sleep this late. Please come in. I want you to stay." I step aside to let him enter, subconsciously running my fingers through my hair. There's still a ton of hairspray from the blowout, so I find tangles and a matted mess. "I must look a complete disaster."

He bends down and kisses me on the forehead. "Never. You look beautiful as always." He sets his coffee down on the side table along with his keys, then takes a wrapped package from his pocket. He looks me over carefully and smiles. "You look like you got a good night's sleep. I brought coffee for you and a treat for Molly."

I smile at him. "That's why she's going crazy."

He holds out two of her favorite dog biscuits from our regular coffee shop, and Molly slathers him with kisses. I don't think anyone could love Dillon more than Molly.

"I think today is going to be the day she goes home with you."

He lets out a deep belly laugh. "She can come home with me any time her mom does." Handing me a cup of coffee, he asks, "What would you like to do today?"

"I was up late running through all the things weighing on my mind. The list is long, but I think I could sleep soundly last night because my subconscious knew about the video and was worried about it. You took care of it, so I finally slept well." I pull him down for a chaste kiss. "I promise to show my deeper appreciation after I brush my teeth."

"Seeing you smile is enough. Unless of course I can talk you into getting away next weekend and head to Denver to see your family? It might be nice to see them."

I'm still not sure. I want to introduce Dillon to my family, but what will I do if he decides to break my heart again? I see he's hopeful that I'll say yes. I guess I need to take a chance and go for it.

Before I can tell him that, he says, "Emerson, I know the last time we were together I behaved incredibly poorly. I promise I'll never do that again."

He's trying hard. I smile and agree. "All right, let's go. I'll see if I can find a pet sitter for Molly. When do you want to go?"

His eyes light up, and I can tell he's excited. "Let's escape early on Friday. We can go directly from the Jamison Technologies presentation."

"I'll have to call my parents and see if they'll be around this weekend. They like to go up in the mountains this time of year."

"I've already talked to your mom. She's arranging dinner on Saturday night, and I've organized a Rockies game on Sunday."

I smile at him. "I see you've sweet-talked your way into my family's heart." I grab Molly's leash and stop. "Wait! How did you get tickets to the game?"

"Easy. Our biggest client has box seats, and I asked for them."

"Box seats at Coors Field? You know they're going to put pressure on you to get serious with me."

"I'll make plans for Bronco box seats this fall if that's what it takes. Besides, no pressure on me. I'm ready. It's you they'll pressure."

My eyes widen. "You're right! You're making it hard to say no."

"Wearing you down is my plan. So, how about a weekend away with your family and me?"

"Sounds like just what we need."

He reaches for my hand and gives it a reassuring squeeze. "What would you like to do today?"

"Let's take Molly down to the bistro for breakfast and the newspaper. After, if you don't mind, I'd like to work on the Jamison presentation and, if time permits, the Page Software presentation since it's the following week."

"Sounds like a perfect plan."

We spend the morning at a local bistro down the street from my house. They have the best eggs benedict, and more importantly there are outside tables where Molly can sun herself at our feet.

As we walk back to my house, I reach for him, and we continue hand in hand. I know it isn't a huge step, but it's in the right direction.

As we work together from my living room, Dillon's phone rings. CeCe is calling to inform him that we have dinner plans with her parents tonight, and if he's man enough, he's welcome to join us. Laughing, he agrees.

Turning to me, he says, "I met her dad years ago when he was a guest lecturer at Stanford. He seemed like a great guy. This should be fun."

I assure him it will be, but warn him that he's like my second dad and CeCe's twin brother, Trey, is like yet another brother for me. "So be prepared to pass inspection."

"I'll win them over as a practice before I meet your own dad and brothers."

DILLON

C ECE PICKS US UP in her Range Rover, Molly joining us in the back seat. When we first met, I didn't put two and two together. It wasn't until later that I realized who CeCe was. She may be Silicon Valley royalty, but you'd never know it when you meet her. She isn't a drama queen, she isn't demanding, and I appreciate how loyal of a friend she is to Emerson.

When we arrive at CeCe's parents, both her mom and dad are standing on the front porch with a small herd of dogs at their feet, all of which are going crazy. Molly joins the frenzy from the back of CeCe's car, the barking and excitement almost deafening.

After we get out and the dogs have the chance to greet one another and calm down, CeCe's dad invites me back to his library. My stomach turns, and I feel like I've been called to the principal's office. We met briefly when you guest lectured at Stanford my sophomore year," I tell him. "You spoke about what made some start-ups succeed and others fail."

"I give that lecture often. Did it make a difference?"

I stand straighter as he hands me a glass of amber liquid.

"Yes, sir, it did. I changed my major to finance with a minor in computer science and a lot of business classes."

He nods. "CeCe tells me you're one of the founders of SHN?"

"I'm the H in SHN."

"Impressive. I've watched you guys have some significant growth. You have an interesting and fresh approach to how you invest."

"Coming from you, sir, that's quite a compliment."

"You did invest in Emerson's company. That says a lot, too."

"We did. But like all of our decisions, it was made by the team. We make sure all partners have an equal say in all of our investments."

"Clever. I've invested over the years in several companies but always on my own. You guys are much smarter about how you go about investing than I ever was. You only use your own money, right?"

"That's how we started. Each time one of our investments sells or goes public, we reward ourselves, but we actually reinvest most of the money into other companies and growing our offerings. Though I don't know that we're any smarter than you are at investing. You backed some of the biggest companies in The Valley when they were starting out." I pause for a second, thinking about my next words. "I almost lost it all recently. I lost my dad almost a year ago, and it was the worst thing that's ever happened to me. It was so bad I almost ruined my relationship with Emerson and lost my position at SHN."

Nodding, he sips his drink. "So what are you going to do about it?"

"Emerson tells me you're a second father to her. I'm here today to get your permission to take her home to her parents and brothers to ask their permission to marry Emerson. That's if she'll have me, of course."

Looking at me closely, he asks, "Have you ever met any of the Winthrop clan?"

"No, sir. Any insight?" I take a deep pull of my drink, trying to hide my nervousness about his answer.

He laughs. "No, but tonight will be a cake walk compared to them, and we're tough. Emerson is the light of her brothers' lives. They won't be easy. Just don't let them take you hunting. Chances are you may not come back."

I blanch at the thought.

"Let's go find the girls," he says, clapping me on the back. "Dillon, you impress me with your knowledge and confidence. Good luck in Boulder."

As WE HEAD BACK after dinner, I'm excited. "Thank you for including me tonight, CeCe."

Looking in her rearview mirror, she tells me, "I knew my dad would love you. I understand you're headed to Boulder next weekend?"

"We are," I say with more confidence than I feel.

"Great, so the following weekend you'll have to report back to all of us on how it goes. That's if Emerson's brothers don't take you hunting."

"I can't wait. But why does everyone keep talking about hunting?"

EMERSON

THE WEEK HAS FLOWN BY, and our covert presentation to Jamison goes exceptionally well. Both sides walk away with the agreement that we'll fund them for four rounds and an eventual forty-eight-percent ownership at a total of two hundred and fifty million dollars.

As we head to the airport for our flight to Denver, my nervousness grows. Dillon is the first guy I've ever seriously brought home. This may well turn into a disaster, but I know if anyone can manage my brothers, Dillon can.

As we exit to Arrivals, I see my mom standing there. She looks like a modern-day hippie, her blonde hair graying and short, which brings out the curls, along with her khaki capris and a tie-dye T-shirt. Standing next to her, my dad's in jeans, cowboy boots, and a shirt advertising an environmentally friendly company he owns outside of his teaching. Then I see them, all four of my brothers standing together in jeans, T-shirts, boots, and baseball caps with their arms crossed over their chests.

Good grief! This weekend is going to be a challenge.

Behind my brothers is the rest of the Winthrop clan—twenty-two people total—to inspect Dillon. If he doesn't run from this, he may be worth keeping.

I give hugs first to my mom and dad, then to each of my brothers and their wives. Once I hug all of my family, I announce, "Everyone, I'd like you to meet my...." I realize I don't know what to call him.

Dillon looks at me and says, "Boyfriend." Turning toward my family, he introduces himself. "I'm her boyfriend, Dillon Healy."

He shakes hands with my dad first, and my mom brings him in for a big hug. He then shakes each of my brothers' hands. They scowl at him, and he takes it all in stride.

Looking at the large group of people, I ask, "How did you all get here?"

My six-year-old nephew Daniel steps forward and proudly says, "We caravanned from Nanna and Pop-pop's."

"Really? Are you all coming over to their house tonight for dinner, or is this it?"

"Yep, we're all coming for dinner. We wanted to check out the asshole."

I close my eyes. *Please tell me Daniel didn't just refer to Dillon as an asshole.*

My mom steps in as everyone, including Dillon, laughs at the honesty of a young child. "I'm sorry. We don't mean to overwhelm you both. We were all just so excited you were coming for a visit."

Getting down on a knee so he can be close in height to Daniel, Dillon tells him, "I've been known to be an asshole, but if

I'm lucky enough, your Auntie Em will allow me to be your Uncle Asshole."

Daniel, with his big brown eyes, puts his arms around Dillon's neck and says for everyone, loud and clear, "I'd like you to be my Uncle Asshole."

WE PILE into my parents' car, and I see my brothers' four vehicles following behind.

"You think you could have left the boys at home to meet up with us later?" I ask.

My dad, looking at me through the rearview mirror, replies, "Well, we tried, but they wanted to meet the first guy you're bringing home."

"You do realize they're the reason I've never brought anyone home, right?" I gently remind them.

My mom quickly interjects, "Dillon, don't let them intimidate you. They're harmless."

"As harmless as baby rattlesnakes—quick and highly venomous," I mutter.

Dillon grabs my hand to reassure me. I know my brothers mean well, but they're overprotective and overbearing. If it were up to them, I'd live in a convent.

As we make our drive from the airport to Boulder, I'm reminded of what I miss about this place. "The sky seems bluer here at altitude."

Dillon shares, "I've never been to Colorado. Not only does the sky seem bluer, but I think the sun is brighter."

"That's because you live in a gray concrete jungle," my dad says.

VENTURE CAPITALIST · FORBIDDEN LOVE

We pull into my parents' current driveway, facing a Victorian house painted vibrant colors that look very similar to my mom's tie-dye shirt. "Wow! This is a project."

"It has great bones, and it may be the one we finally stay in as soon as we finish refurbishing it." My mom smiles while staring at the house.

I chuckle and tell Dillon, "They've said that about the last three houses they've lived in."

As everyone arrives and my family files out of their minivans and SUVs, a happy chaos erupts: kids running around and playing, dogs barking, my brothers and Dillon surrounding a big-screen television, watching the Rockies game and drinking beer. I help my mom and sisters-in-law with dinner. Mom has been slow-cooking a brisket all day, and the girls have side dishes, salads, vegetables, and desserts. You would think this is enough food to feed an army of a hundred men. We'll see if there are any leftovers.

I hear the baseball game on the television, and the guys are peppering Dillon with questions about our relationship and his intentions. He handles them well. I'm impressed.

"I like Dillon, sweetie," my mom tells me.

I smile at her, a bit embarrassed. "Thanks, Mom. So do I. I just hope the guys don't scare him off."

Smiling like a cat who just caught a canary, she says, "Oh, somehow I don't think that will be an issue."

Everything is finally laid out, and my mom yells, "Dinner's on the table!"

We all pile into the dining room, the table expanded to seat all two dozen of us. My dad leads us in the Catholic grace. When he's done, my sister-in-law June asks, "Are you Catholic, Dillon?"

"I am," he tells her, and she smiles. That's two of my family members down in the Dillon column—only twenty more to go.

As the evening wears on, each person asks Dillon questions, and he answers them with skill, never breaking a sweat.

My sixteen-year-old niece Jessica has watched the conversation and finally asks, "Auntie Em, do you love Dillon?"

Everyone turns to me and waits expectantly. I look at Dillon and, with more authority than I feel, state, "I do. Very, very much."

THE REMAINDER OF THE WEEKEND is a blur. My parents torture Dillon with a hike in Rocky Mountain National Park on Saturday. Both talk about the environmental issues which are important to them, and Dillon listens intently asking questions as if he's a potential investor. My older brother has everyone over for a barbecue. On Sunday after brunch, we head to the Rockies game and watch them beat the Dodgers. Full of hot dogs, popcorn, pretzels, and a few glasses of beer, everyone is having a grand time.

After the game, it's time to head back to the Bay Area. My brothers are all smiles and shake Dillon's hand, and my sisters-in-law all hug him goodbye. He's passed all their tests with flying colors.

My oldest brother, Nick, pulls me aside and says, "He's a good guy, Emmy. I hope we'll see him again."

I wipe tears from my eyes. "Thank you. I love you guys. Come visit us soon."

ONCE WE GET SETTLED at the airport, Dillon leans in close. "Thank you for sharing your family with me. I think they liked me."

Squeezing his knee, I kiss him softly on the lips. "I don't think. I know they do. They didn't offer to take you hunting after all," I giggle.

"So, can we get away next weekend to Napa, just the two of us?"

Snuggling close, I tell him, "I think I would like that as long as we make it back to the Arnaults' in Hillsboro for dinner Sunday night."

He kisses the top of my head.

I feel comfortable. Happy. Loved. I'm not perfect, but I'd follow him into Hell if that's what it took to keep him safe. I'm his protector as he is mine, one to shield the other. Not a single soul or our jobs comes before him. I'll stay with him as he stays with me, trust in him as he trusts in me, and together we'll ride through every storm, waiting to see what the new dawn may bring.

DILLON

W E WORK APART for the week, spend our evenings together. I secretly make plans for our weekend in Napa.

I pick her up at her bungalow after work, where she emerges in tight jeans, a clingy red sweater, a black leather jacket that hugs her curves, and high-heeled black leather boots. Holding an overnight bag in one hand and a garment bag in the other, she's ready to go.

My palms are sweating. I'm nervous for our weekend. So much is riding on how everything goes.

We watch the sun set over the Golden Gate Bridge as we drive up the 101 to Napa, the beautiful orange sun dropping over the wide expanse of the Pacific Ocean.

I reach for her hand and say, "Thank you for coming with me this weekend."

She smiles at me. "I wouldn't have missed this for anything."

As nervous as I've been for our weekend away, I feel a calmness from her touch. I hope we have a fun weekend.

WHEN WE ARRIVE at the Spanish-style hotel, the valets are quick to meet us and help us unload the car. The property surrounding the hotel is covered in acres of grapes, paired with a beautiful cacophony of color from the blooms on the rose bushes at the end of each row. Each hotel suite is a bungalow surrounded by green grass and flower beds with fragrant lavender bushes in full purple blooms.

We're handed glasses of champagne as we check in, and the bellmen prepares to escort us to our rooms. As we walk through the courtyards, he points out the restaurants, spa, pools, workout rooms, yoga studio, and business center. I'll never remember what's where, but I don't think many of those locations are on our agenda this weekend. Honestly, I hope we spend most of the time in our room.

When we arrive at our suite, the bellmen gives us a tour. I don't hear a thing they say after they point out the fire burning in the fireplace. I see the bottle of California sparkling wine and bowl of chocolate-covered strawberries I ordered next to the fireplace. The plush rug and big pillows nearby are perfect for fireside lovemaking. The bellman realizes he's lost our attention and quickly leaves.

I turn to look at Emerson and see the awe on her face. Every time I see her, she's even more beautiful. The golden glow of the fire only heightens her exquisiteness. My cock, which has been hard for hours, is anxious for some play. "There's a Jacuzzi tub. Would you like to join me for a bath?"

She nods and begins taking her clothes off. I can't wait, crossing the room in two broad steps and kissing her senseless. Pulling back, she removes her boots, socks, and jeans, leaving her in a sweater and very sexy black panties. She slides her arms around my neck and flattens herself against my front before tilting her head up and capturing my lips. She takes every bit of what I'm giving and meets me with a hot passion that leaves me needy.

Leaning forward, I brush my nose along hers, wanting to take things slow, and yet not. Moving down and pressing my mouth and nose to her sex, breathing in deeply and then glancing up at Emerson as she stiffens. Her eyes close as I flick my tongue over her panty-covered mound.

"God," she groans and pushes my head away. "Too much."

I take her wrist in my hand and lick along the inside of her thigh. "Not nearly enough. Relax and let me taste you."

She's almost shaking by the time I tug her sexy panties off. I splay my fingers over her stomach as I push her sweater up. Her nipples are hard and wanting as they strain against her bra, and she arches her back into me as I play with the hard nubs. Trapping my hand against her breast, she opens her legs as she beckons me to enjoy her wet slit.

She tastes like honey, and I lap up everything she offers. My fingers probe her tight channel as I lick and taste, her muscles grasping and holding me inside. I hum to cause a slight vibration and she moans out her pleasure, filling my mouth with more of her sweet honey.

She's the whole deal, the perfect woman as far as I'm concerned. It's scary to think that something so close to perfection is in my grasp, and yet there's a high chance I could very well fuck it all up this weekend.

I lead her to the tub, which smells of lavender, and quickly undress so we can climb in together, sitting opposite of each other. Mirrors cover the walls around us, and it's very erotic. Her nipples peek at me from the water as she starts the jets, and I take her foot in my hands, massaging one and then the other. She leans back and moans, making my cock hard as a baseball bat, peeking out of the water.

Opening her eyes, she sees it waving at her and smiles. "I think our friend is looking for some attention."

I lift my hips and she bends over, taking my cock deep into her mouth, swirling her tongue around the hard, bulbous head while stroking my balls. She swallows me deep in her mouth, going up and down while looking right at me. I watch, enraptured, feeling her tongue flatten so she can take more of my length deep into her throat. When she pulls up, she flicks at the tip. What an incredible sensation.

One hand cups my balls and plays with them while the other holds my cock steady at the base as she moves it in and out of her delicate mouth. She works me slowly and the fire spreads through my veins—pure, hot, unadulterated lust. God help me, I want her. I won't let myself come in her mouth. It's too early in my plans for the evening.

When we exit the tub, I grab a plush white towel and dry her, and she does the same to me. I caress her warm, soft skin as I spoon her by the fire. I whisper in her ear, "I love you, Emerson. I always have, and I always will."

Rolling over to look at me, she says without hesitation, "I love you, Dillon. I always have and always will."

My cock is poking at the apex of her thighs. I roll her on her back, my fingers finding her wet slit. She's wet and ready for me. Lifting her hips up to meet mine, there's a look of need on her face, and I know she's ready. I slide my cock into her slowly, leaning down on my forearms so I can be close to her face, which I intend to cover in kisses.

Warm inside her, our bodies combined, I whisper, "I love you."

I slowly move through her, never wanting to leave. Her pussy hugs my cock perfectly, and with every drive inside her, I want to come. But I ride it out, looking into her eyes and moving slowly, a major tease for us both. I get harder and start slamming my cock into her methodically as her face burns with desire.

We spend long stretches of time in bed feeling each other's skin, running our hands over every inch of the other's body, memorizing curves, lines, and angles. We make love again, and then we fall asleep. We somehow manage to order in room service, which we leisurely enjoy before turning back to each other once again. It's an evening and early morning of love, sex, and sleep, with maybe a little food and a lot of Emerson.

A lot of naked Emerson.

DILLON

$\mathcal{S}$TRETCHING IN BED as the sun rises, I'm comforted by how good Emerson feels in my arms. I want her with me always.

Ordering breakfast in, we enjoy a slow and relaxing morning. My next surprise to our weekend begins when there's a knock at our door. Two masseurs come into our suite and set up their tables next to each other by the fire. They light candles with a seductive vanilla and lavender scent, and we enjoy our ninety-minute couples massage.

After they leave, we're relaxed and enjoying our time together. We make love again, slow and sensual, each stroke pulling out another level of pleasure until I'm sure I'll pass out. I've never been as happy.

When we dress for dinner, my eyes move down her taut back to the curve of her ass, memorizing her sexiness and trying to talk myself out of reaching out and doing something that would surely prevent the evening I've planned.

I've ordered the hotel's car service, wanting to look at her every moment I can. I don't want to miss anything. As Emerson crosses the hotel lobby and enters the car, I see she's captured the eye of every man in the vicinity. She's stunning with her long legs, stiletto sandals, and emerald-green shift dress that hugs every curve, straining across her chest. Her hair is curled and piled high on her head, soft tendrils strategically falling around her face. She has a glow of happiness and contentment. She isn't just beautiful, she's stunning.

Giving me a million-dollar smile, she asks, "Where are we going?"

Smiling back, I reach for her hand, intertwining our fingers and squeezing gently. Bringing her hand to my mouth, I softly kiss it as she rests her head on my shoulder.

I've used my connections to get us a table at The French Laundry, a Michelin three-star restaurant. It's considered by some to be the best in all of North and South America. I've only been here one other time, and it was probably the greatest meal I've ever had. It's a destination restaurant for fine French cuisine in the Napa Valley, located in a rustic two-story stone cottage with a quaint courtyard.

We have the eight o'clock seating and will enjoy the tasting menu. As we walk in, we're greeted by the host, dressed in a well-tailored coat and tie, by name. "Monsieur Healy and Ma-demoiselle Winthrop. Welcome to The French Laundry." Walking us to our table in the quiet restaurant, which is immaculate in design and filled with exquisite smells of spices and fine aromas, he seats us in a high-back booth so we're able to sit next to rather than across from one another. Much more intimate. "Phillipe will be your lead server, with Ramone and Francesca supporting him this evening, and Jennifer, our sommelier, will be with you shortly. May I offer you a bottle of sparkling water?"

My fingers are on her thigh as I run small circles around it, inching higher and higher up her leg. "Yes, please."

As we sit together in the restaurant, I let my eyes move down the thickness of her bottom lip, remembering how good it feels pressed against mine. She tastes like passion and feels like heaven.

The tasting menu comes as an eight-course meal, each only a little bit more than a taste, and I've preordered wine paired with each one. It's a different half glass for each of us, so we can remember our dinner. The ambiance is romantic, with a slight tinkle of piano keys that can be heard through the auspiciously placed speakers and the low lighting adding to the intimacy of a romantic dinner.

The raw oyster starter arrives with two delicious oysters on a half shell sprinkled with white sturgeon caviar. The sommelier places a cold half glass of 2015 Bevan Cellars Sauvignon Blanc before each of us, and we toast. "To us," I say. We tip the small oysters into our mouths, tasting almost like pure butter as it slips down my throat. Emerson closes her eyes and gives the most delicious moan, which is extremely arousing.

We talk about how the first two presentations have gone well and the confidence we have in securing them without issue.

"I wonder how Perkins Klein is doing with the other four companies," Emerson says.

"I almost feel bad that we have our team running circles to deceive them."

"Me, too."

The waitstaff soundlessly arrive delivering the second course: a duck foie gras soup paired with the 2011 Epoch Estate Wines Syrah. I love watching her enjoy the soup. When a small drip hits her chin, I want to lean over and lick it off.

She smiles at me as she wipes her chin. "This is delicious. I can taste layers of the soup--the duck foie gras, butter, a jolt of cognac-kissed smoothness." Breathing in deeply, she continues, "There's a pungent, earthy silkiness. This is magnificent. I've never had anything like it before. It's rich, and absolutely divine!"

Phillipe asks if we've enjoyed the second course, and I joke, "It was terrible, as you can see. We've literally licked the bowls."

Emerson and I talk about her friends. I'm surprised Greer works in marketing for a start-up that recently has a lot of buzz as it's been announced that it'll be acquired by Microsoft.

"Why didn't I know she was working for them?"

She shrugs. "I guess she never mentioned it when you were around. She's had some great stories of how they've been behaving and all the trouble she's bailed them out of. She's a little bit disappointed to be out of a job, but she has a significant interest in the company and will take some time off before she looks for other work."

"Given she worked for that company, we may have a client who can use her. Would you mind working with her professionally?"

"Absolutely not! I think she's a marketing genius, and we would be lucky if she were part of some of our investments."

The third course arrives with a beautiful 2005 Peter Michael Winery Chardonnay along with what's called the Mediterranean

John Dory. It's a light, firm, and flaky white fish that is delicate on the palate.

"The fish essentially melts in your mouth as you eat. It's gorgeous on the plate, and taking a bite is like destroying art, but the wonderful smell wafting from the plate makes it difficult to resist.

Every course improves over the last. How is it possible?"

"I'm glad you're enjoying yourself."

She nods as she savors every bite like it's her last. "Definitely."

"You impressed my family when you met them at the wake and funeral, so we're even."

"I very much doubt they remember me beyond being one of the partners in your firm."

"You know, when Celeste was starting her craziness, my mom asked about you. Did you tell her I stayed in your room at the Townsend?"

"Goodness, no! She's a good Catholic. I know better."

"Somehow she knew. She likes you."

"Well, that's good. We'll have to make a trip out to visit your mom soon."

"I've promised my sister and mom that I'd come scatter my dad's ashes later this summer. We want to go on a boat to Mackinac Island. Will you come with me?"

"Of course, but that's a very intimate activity. Are you sure you want me to join you? It's such a private moment."

"I have no doubt that I want you with me. I can't imagine doing anything without you at my side."

She leans in and kisses me. "I love you."

"I love you, too."

As we sit in silence, holding hands, the fourth course is served with the Honig Winery's Sauvignon Blanc. Plated in front of us is a beautiful plump lobster half-tail sautéed with chili flakes and placed on a bed of watercress with a hint of lemon. Moaning while enjoying the delicious course, Emerson says, "It's fresh, vibrant, and crunchy, with enough spicy zing to wake us up."

"I don't think I've ever had lobster served like this. Have you?"

"Amazing," she agrees.

As they clear the course, she carefully asks, "Have you heard anything from Adam?"

I shake my head. "No. Have you?"

"Oh God no!" After a few seconds of silence, she asks, "It occurred to me that he might have shared the videos he made with others. Do we know anything about that?"

"According to the black hat, he did share them with the one other guy, but we don't know their connection. We believe he was his partner and possible drug dealer, so we've also gone after him the same way we did Adam." Stroking her arm, I look at her intently. "We don't think the video exists anywhere else."

"Have I told you recently how much I love you?"

"You can tell me that all day, every day if you'd like."

Smiling, she says, "I think I'll do that."

The fifth course arrives, the truffle selection which includes a generous serving of white truffles grated over risotto, paired with the 2013 J. Wilkes Santa Maria Valley Pinot Noir. Emerson continues to groan and enjoy our meal. "Wow! This risotto is nothing like I've ever tasted. Such a wild array of textures: an airy crunch at the edges, and the softer grain of the rice with rolling bubbles of flavor populated by the truffles, creating pockets of perfection skittering across the surface."

I laugh. "You should be a food critic."

She shakes her head. "I would be huge. But honestly, this has been the best meal I've ever had. Thank you for making this special."

My heart warms at her endearment. "It's only special because we're here together."

Leaning in, she kisses me deeply. Our lips part and our tongues dance a soft romantic ballet.

I want to know everything about her, all of her hopes and dreams. "If you could go anywhere, where would you go?" I ask her.

"Wow! That's a tough question. I'd like to explore so many places. I think there's something on every continent that I want to one day see and do. What about you?"

"I'd love to explore where my dad is from in Ireland. We went when we were kids, but I hardly remember it. I want to go see the polar bears in the wild in the Arctic Circle. I want to take a boat down the Amazon. I guess I also have a long list of things I want to do on every continent."

"You're a romantic at heart you, know." I nod at her and she asks, "Would you ever do any of those things alone?"

"I think I've been waiting for someone to join me who wants to do those things as much as I do."

She holds my hand and we snuggle in close to one another. It all just feels right.

We have three more courses to go and now are ready for the two meat courses. Starting the sixth course, they place a natural-fed veal alongside Yukon Gold potatoes, baby red beets, Brussels sprouts, horseradish créme fraîche, and a sauce borscht, paired with the 1999 Screaming Eagle Cabernet Sauvignon.

I'm the first to moan this time. "Wow. The veal is tender yet moist and juicy."

Nodding enthusiastically, Emerson says, "It has an earthy texture and is obviously grass-fed."

"You can tell that?"

She chuckles. "I believe so, yes."

"I would bet you can tell all the different scents and tastes with each of the wines, too."

"I'm not as good with wines as I am with foods. You have to remember, when I was growing up, there were five kids—and four of them ate enormous amounts of food. We rarely could afford to go out, so my mom made dinner most nights. As the years went on, she became an incredible cook. I loved cooking with her."

"I can't wait for you to make something for me."

"I've cooked for you, haven't I?"

"Not really. But we have plenty of time for that."

"I promise a good homemade meal soon."

As we enjoy ourselves and the conversation, the seventh course arrives at the table and is absolutely stunning, both visually and in taste. It's a slice of lamb, the meat aged to perfection, nicely marbled and roasted with golden and buttery pomme frites, paired with a 1996 Colgin Cellars Cabernet Sauvignon.

When she finishes the last morsel, Emerson says, "This is another amazing course. Each time I think they can't do better, they do."

"I can see why this is thought to be the best restaurant in all of the Americas."

"I think I've had eight glasses of water, but I can't be sure because every time I put my glass down, they fill it up again. With that, if you'll excuse me, I need to find the ladies' room."

I stand up with her as she walks to the bathroom. She's the most beautiful woman in the entire restaurant tonight.

The sommelier comes over and asks me about the wine selections.

"They've been the perfect accompaniment. Thank you," I tell her.

"Well, you did pick them out yourself. You have excellent taste."

"Thank you. I hope others are able to enjoy them, too."

"They are, without a doubt."

Emerson returns and she looks refreshed. "I see you were talking to the sommelier. Is she happy with your wine pairings?"

"How did you know I chose them?"

She laughs. "Because first of all, these are entirely too nice of wines even for this restaurant to go with a tasting menu, and second, I know you."

Leaning over, I quickly kiss her nose. "I hate being predictable."

She laughs the most melodious sound as they place the eighth and final course in front of us. Paired with a glass of Johnny Walker Blue Label eighteen-year-old blended scotch whiskey, each of us enjoys an order of the profiteroles served with ice cream in a beautiful and intricate design on the plate.

Sighing, she says, "The shattering, airy crunch of meringue at the edges and the softer one of toasted almonds are just fantastic together."

To end our epicurean extravaganza, we enjoy the restaurant's signature cinnamon-sugared doughnuts, which are thick, gooey, and deliciously warm alongside a hot frothy decaf coffee. "I know I've probably been too loud in my appreciation of the food tonight, but I really want to thank you for dinner. It has been amazing to eat, and more importantly share with you."

Phillipe arrives at the table. "Monsieur Healy, Mademoiselle Winthrop, Chef Keller is hoping you'd like to join him for a tour of the kitchen."

Emerson looks at me expectantly, nodding. "Please?"

Turning to Phillipe, I chuckle. "I think that's a yes."

It's after midnight, and the few employees who remain in the kitchen are doing the final wipe-down of all the stainless-steel tables, the dishwashers busy running dishes. "Dillon!"

"Chef Keller. I'd like to introduce you to my girlfriend, Emerson Winthrop."

"So nice to meet you," Emerson says as she extends her hand.

Chef Keller reaches out and brings her hand to his mouth for a kiss. "Enchanté, vous avez très belle.

"Merci, le dîner était incroyable."

"Vous parlez français magnifique avec un accent de Paris, oui?"

"Mais oui, j'ai étudié le français à Stanford et à la Sorbonne."

In a thick French accent, Chef Keller says, "Dillon, you have a very talented woman here. She loves French food and speaks fluent French like a Parisian."

Looking at her with surprise, I state, "I'm not letting her out of my sight!"

"Your kitchen is beautiful, and the food was beyond outstanding. Phillipe, Ramone, and Francesca were all fantastic. I can see how you've earned the perfect Michelin star rating," Emerson gushes.

"I'm glad you enjoyed yourself. Please feel free to extend your dining experience to our courtyard. I'd love to treat you to a rare cognac and pre-embargo Cuban cigar," he offers.

We sit quietly in the courtyard. Her eyes grow heavy as we drink a glass of a rare cognac that I didn't catch the name of when Chef Keller delivered it. I considered one of the cigars but I was afraid it might limit my options later. Leaning in, "I'm ready to get you back to our hotel room and make sweet love to you all night long."

DILLON

W E MAKE LOVE TWICE before going to sleep wrapped around each other, the second time far slower. I've never made love to a woman like that, but after doing it, I could see why. It's like I lost a piece of myself with every thrust, every moan, every whimper she let out. She's impossibly beautiful, a treasure I want to hide away from the world.

I've been with lots of girls, but no one makes me feel the way Emerson does. She makes love to me with passion like nothing I've ever experienced. It isn't about getting off or seeing who could make the other person scream more, but about taking her time to show me the depths of her heart with her body.

"Emerson, I love you so much."

"I love you, too."

Reaching into the nightstand, I pull out my grandmother's ring, then sit her up and drop to one knee. "Emerson, you're the center of my universe. I love you more than words can express. You've helped me through my darkest moments, and you still love me. It would make me the happiest man in the world if you would be my wife."

"I love you, too. Only you. Forever."

Wiping tears from her eyes, I press my lips to hers.

EMERSON

$\mathcal{I}$T'S A MILDLY WARM fall day, the sky dotted with a few pillow clouds—perfect for a carnival. For those arriving, the entrance can be seen in the distance, and the long lines of clients, employees and their families edge forward slowly as they work their way in. Faint music can be heard from beyond the tall gates, with the occasional happy scream suddenly piercing the air. Closer to the entrance, the massive structures of the rides can be seen: a rollercoaster, a Ferris wheel, and helter-skelter. The sounds of elephants trumpeting and a lion's roar add to the excitement.

Entering the event, young children stand watching, eating their sweets and snacks. Ice creams wobbling perilously over the cones and dripping down their small fingers as they melt. Some munch on brightly colored soft sugar strands of cotton candy which dissolve on the tongue—sweeter than sweet and sticking to the teeth better than glue. Others enjoy white puffs of buttery popcorn.

Our fall carnival is a place of unrestrained joy for everyone of all ages. Tina completely outdid herself. The costumes of the carnival staff light up the fall day. Dressed as clowns, they are a mixture of color to rival any gardener's paradise. Music fills the air, festive beats to lift the spirits and make the people want to move, jump, and sing. It's a time to celebrate being alive, enjoy the wonders of creation, and be one with the community our company has created. The air tastes heavenly with the chefs of the dozens of colorful food trucks alongside the edge of our event. Every delicious thing ready to be shared with friends and conversations to be had with families.

The clowns sport crazy-colored wigs, flawless porcelain-white faces, and mouths made three times their original size in red. Their eyes are lined with black as smoothly as if painted by an artist, and each has different decoration on their cheeks, such as a glittered star, a colorful rainbow, and big red hearts. Dressed in oversized clothes and shoes, they smile into the crowds, and the crowds smile back. Some hand out large vibrantly colored balloons filled with helium, others make balloon animals and hats, and still others lead small animals to be pet by young children.

Most people wander from food truck to food truck, sampling street tacos, hot dogs, hamburgers, funnel cakes, fried Twinkies, and skewered meats. Mason, Dillon, and Cameron greet our clients, employees, and their family members as they wander through the throngs of people.

This party has far outdone anything we've ever managed before. Our fall picnic is the only time of the year where the day is long but the night is even longer. There's a stage where six bands play live music, rotating through the day and into the evening as people of all ages dance to the mesmerizing beats.

Mason sees me and walks over. "Emerson, you and your team outdid yourselves. This is an incredible fall picnic."

I smile from ear to ear. "Thank you, Mason. Wendy's sister did all this under budget and at no cost to us. She did it only in return for a reference from us."

"Make sure we give her a top-notch reference. Everyone is having a great time, the food is fantastic, and the rides are the cherry on an ice cream sundae."

"I'd like to offer her a generous tip. We can discuss it at the partners meeting next week."

"If it all continues this well, I don't think you'll have any problem convincing us."

Over the roar of music, a distant, hazy chatter can be heard. I can't make out any words, but laughter rings in my ears and won't seem to stop. The song gets louder, pulling me in, and won't let go. I have no choice but to join the crowd dancing to a nineties hair band, jumping in a huddled group like Tic-Tacs being shaken in a box.

Reaching for my hand, Dillon kisses me. "I love you."

Turning to him, I murmur, "I love you, forever and always."

Thank you !

Thanks for reading *Venture Capitalist: Forbidden Love.* I do hope you enjoyed Dillon and Emerson's story and reading the first in the Venture Capitalist series. I appreciate your help in spreading the word, including telling a friend. Before you go, it would mean so much to me if you would take a few minutes to write a review and capture how you feel about what you've read so others may find my work. Reviews help readers find books. Please leave a review on your favorite book site.

Don't miss out on New Releases, Exclusive Giveaways and much more!

- Join Ainsley's **newsletter**

- Like Ainsley St Claire on **Facebook:**
  https://www.facebook.com/ainsleystclaire/?noti f_id=1513620809190446&notif_t=page_admin

- Join Ainsley's **reader group:**
  www.ainsleystclaire.com

- Follow Ainsley St Claire on **Twitter**:
  https://twitter.com/AinsleyStClaire

- Follow Ainsley St Claire on **Pinterest**:
  https://www.pinterest.ca/ainsleystclaire/

- Follow Ainsley St Claire on **Goodreads**:
  https://www.goodreads.com/author/show/1675
  2271.Ainsley_St_Claire

- Follow Ainsley St Claire on **Reddit**:
  https://www.ainsleystclaire.com/www.reddit.co
  m/user/ainsleystclaire

- Visit Ainsley's website for her current **booklist**:
  www.ainsleystclaire.com

I love to hear from you directly, too. Please feel free to **email** me at ainsley@ainsleystclaire.com or check out my **website** www.ainsleystclaire.com for updates.

Other Books
by Ainsley St Claire

If you loved *Venture Capitalist: Forbidden Love,* you may enjoy the other sensual, sexy and romantic stories and books she has published.

The Golf Lesson
(An Erotic Short Story)

In a Perfect World

About
Ainsley

Ainsley St Claire is a Denver-based Contemporary Romance Author and Adventurer on a lifelong mission to craft sultry storylines and steamy love scenes that captivate her readers. To date, she is best known for her debut "naughty Nicholas Sparks" novel entitled "In A Perfect World".

An avid reader since the age of four, Ainsley's love of books knew no genre. After reading, came her love of writing, fully immersing herself in the colorful, impassioned world of contemporary romance.

Ainsley's passion immediately shifted to a vocation when during a night of terrible insomnia, her first book came to her. Ultimately, this is what inspired her to take that next big step. The moment she wrote her first story, the rest was history.

Currently, Ainsley is in the midst of writing her Venture Capitalist series.

When she isn't being a bookworm or typing away her next story on her computer, Ainsley enjoys spending quality family time with her loved ones. She is happily married to her amazing soulmate and is a proud mother of two rambunctious boys. She is also a scotch aficionada and lover of good food (especially melt-in-your-mouth, velvety chocolate). Outside of books, family, and food, Ainsley is a professional sports spectator and an equally as terrible golfer and tennis player.

Made in the USA
San Bernardino, CA
24 February 2018